SECRET LIVES

SECRET LIVES

S. J. Brown

To order additional copies of this book, contact:
Xlibris Corporation
0-800-644-6988
www.xlibrispublishing.co.uk
Orders@xlibrispublishing.co.uk
307048

1

NINA.

Beep! Beep! Beep! Nina rolled over and slammed her alarm clock off. 7am already. She felt like she had just laid her head to rest on her pillow. The weekend had disappeared into oblivion in a matter of seconds before Monday morning arrived knocking at her door impatiently.

Nina gazed out of her bedroom window lying amidst a mountain of cushions and pillows. Her bed was her sanctuary, the place she felt safe, sound and calm. The place she gathered her thoughts and confronted her fears. The place where she felt relaxed and assessed her life.

She worked as a Personnel Assistant to Mr Allen, a man she maintained a love hate relationship with out of necessity as he provided her with her with an income that enabled her to pay her bills for her little two bed roomed flat in Moseley, to run her Mini Cooper and to enjoy a handful of fun in her spare time.

Nina was a straight girl, very prim and proper, if she let her hair down it was a Kodak moment. At twenty nine years of age, nearing the big three zero, Nina wanted more out of her life. She longed for excitement and fun, a man to show her a good time and treat her right. She was fed up of these good for nothing, no show, all talk, leach off females, pretend to admire independent women, illegal, life living guys!!! She wanted a man with his own independence, who would whisk her off of her feet, a companion, lover, best friend, the blah, blah, blah . . . the nonexistent man so she thought.

She wanted to earn full time wages but with part time hours. Take time to enjoy her life, lunches, dinners, spa dates with the girls, holidays twice a year, bank holiday weekends let alone weekends away. Nice clothes instead of office suits day in day out! Nina had had enough of her, 'simple life.' She wanted change and she wanted it at a five star standard.

Pouring her double 'choca mocha' into her travel mug and then loading up the boot of her car with work files, Nina hadn't even realised how she had gotten out of bed and showered and dressed. Looking at herself she accepted it was due to how routine her life actually was. Pencil skirt, blouse and kitten heels, the same daily attire, yawn, what a bore. With that she hit the pedal to the metal and journeyed up the busy Hagley road to work.

"Good morning Nina." Mr Allen greeted her as she walked through the office.

"Good morning Mr Allen." Nina replied merely glancing in his direction.

She marched straight into her office which was located as a separate room off of Mr Allen's. She placed her workload on her desk and sighed as she sat in her swivel chair mentally preparing herself to plough through the day ahead.

Mr Allen knocked on Nina's office door lightly and lingered in the doorway. Nina looked up at him. "How can I help?" She asked.

"Erm . . . Nina," he began softly "I am conducting a few interviews this morning, one starting in precisely fifteen minutes, so could you refrain from walking through my office whilst it is in progress please? It's just that I do not want any unnecessary distractions. Not that I'm holding you hostage or anything," he said with a chuckle.

Nina arched her eyebrow and looked at Mr Allen curiously. Was this man being serious? Never in the six years Nina had worked for him had he made such a request. She was not stupid. In all the time she had known him, she knew when he was up to something shady. Mr Allen was your typical square man. Spoke the Queen's English, suit starched, sharp jaw etc. He had a wife whom he never spoke about or whom even had presence, not even a photograph on his desk.

Nina granted his request with a laugh, "No problem Mr Allen." She washed her hands and grabbed her fruit pot from the fridge. She resigned to her office making sure she had all she required so as not to cause any 'unnecessary distractions' as Mr Allen put it.

She soon came to realise how serious Mr Allen actually was when he went as far as to close the blinds that divided their window.

Trying to get lost in her work in hope of time picking up its pace, Nina became a little curious at some sounds coming from the other side of her door. Although under strict instructions not to cause a disturbance she couldn't resist and had to at least try and be discretely nosey. She scooted her chair over to the side of her office to where the door was. Placing her ear to the gap she heard a female voice asking Mr Allen what he desired. From Mr Allen came a muffle which Nina could not quite work out. The female voice then went on to mention money. Again a muffled mumble was Mr Allen's response. Nina was lost. What was Mr Allen doing?

It then fell into place.

"Yes baby . . . oh yes . . . just like that . . . mmmhhmm . . ."

That was it. Nina slowly slid the door open a crack and peeped through. She could not believe her eyes. Mr Allen had a tall, plastic fantastic looking 'chick' in just her lingerie and stilettos performing sexual acts for him in his office, on his desk! Mr Allen could not get enough, groping and biting and sucking!

Nina was stunned. So many thoughts ran through her mind at a hundred miles per hour. Why was he doing this? Why use the work vicinity? How dare he lie about interviews when he was enduring a guilty pleasure? Not to mention it was making her horny as hell!

Mr Allen and the chick were so engrossed in the heat of the moment that neither of them were aware in the slightest of Nina's beady eyes watching them.

When all was done, the juices spilled and the sweat mopped up, Nina observed as the 'chick' put her clothes on (a business suit?) powdered her nose and placed a white envelope in her purse. Money?

Nina scooted back over to her desk rapidly and crossed her legs acting as if she had been positioned in that manner for the past hour. She pretended not to even notice when Mr Allen opened the blinds and resumed normal activity as if she was a fool. Lunch time could not come quick enough. The biggest breath of fresh air was a matter of life or death given what she had witnessed in the office that morning.

"I'm going to get some lunch, do you want anything?" Nina asked Mr Allen, avoiding all eye contact. She had seen his private parts and his sexual faces whilst having sex with a stranger like he was totally in the comfort of his own home!

"I'm ok thanks Nina, oh, and thanks for not causing any distractions."

"Wish I could say the same." Nina said thinking she had said it under her breath.

"What was that?" Mr Allen asked.

"I said erm . . . are you sure you wouldn't like anything?"

"I'm fine once again," he replied, and with that Nina walked out of the office with a face like a beetroot.

An hour's lunch break and Nina was going to fulfil every minute of it. She decided on a pub lunch so she chose a quiet spot at a table in the corner of the Harvester where she became one with her book.

Her break didn't last long at all and Nina went to the ladies room to freshen up before returning back to the office. Whilst in the ladies cubicle doing her business Nina heard weird sounds coming from the cubicle right beside hers. Heavy panting and breathing, skin on skin slapping, slurping . . . she propped her hand mirror up on the cubicle floor to discover the same 'chick' from the office that morning giving a guy she recognised from the bar a sexual favour! Flabbergasted she gathered her stuff together and left the cubicle.

Once inside of her car, something wouldn't let Nina drive off easily and she did not know what it was.

Twice in one day she had clapped eyes on the same woman doing the same thing. This woman was dressed like she attended a decent, contemporary job. Instead she was wondering around performing sexual acts and favours for loads of money and no one would have the foggiest idea.

This woman's lifestyle was becoming a little too attractive to Nina. She started thinking along the lines of fun and adventure not to mention money and sex. Safe sex obviously. What was happening to her and why were these thoughts even crossing her mind? How dare they! Was her life that empty? What did she think she was missing?

Nina waited in her car and watched as the 'chick' casually walked over to her Lexus and got in. Anyone would assume she was a working class lady but Nina knew better. Call girl? Prostitute? Escort? Is that working class? Aren't they all the same thing just different names?

Nina decided there and than that she wanted a taste, even if it was just a little bit. Curiosity had gotten the best of her.

Feeling daring and brave she drove towards the 'chicks' car and blocked her in such a way she could not manoeuvre out. She wound her window low and signalled the woman to do the same.

"Excuse me, can I talk to you for a moment please?" Nina hollered at her.

The 'chick' realised she could not go anywhere and was intrigued as to what Nina wanted. She was panicked and tried to disguise it.

"I just want to talk business with you," Nina smiled.

JORDAN.

"Are we good to shag?" Mark asked Jordan lying in the king sized bed with his arms stretched above his head smiling.

For once Jordan longed for a 'normal' morning. She was fed up of checking her temperature and where about she was in her ovulation cycle, all in the name of conceiving. The novelty of having sex twenty four seven had worn off because that is all it had become, shagging!

"I'm fed up Mark!" Jordan snapped. "For once, this Monday morning I want to just get up, shower and dress and go to damn work!" And that's exactly what she did. All the while Mark stood like a statue watching as his frustrated wife stomped around their home huffing and puffing like the 'Big Bad Wolf.'

Mark and Jordan had been married four years after meeting at a school conference. They were both teachers. Jordan an English teacher at a Sixth Form College and Mark a Geography teacher at a Secondary School. Marks mother had planted the idea of children into their heads as she was yearning to be a Grandmother to have something to occupy her time now she was retired and she had applied the pressure long and hard as Mark was her only child.

Jordan loved and admired her husband. They both worked hard not just in their careers but also to maintain a happy home and marriage. Lately the pressure of baby making was taking its toll. Jordan missed her best friend Nina, they were so distant lately. They hardly had their girly nights in let alone out. All of Jordan's spare time was designated to the baby making ritual which she no longer enjoyed. The meaning of Marks touch seemed absent. It lacked sensuality and affection and breathed purpose and task.

Marching through the Sixth Form corridor at fifty miles per hour, Jordan accidentally dropped a few papers, kneeling down to retrieve them she was greeted with a helping hand.

"Here, let me help you Miss."

It was Alec, one of her students.

"Aww thanks Alec you are a star," she replied gratefully, hurriedly gathering as much papers up as she could.

"Are you ok Miss?" Alec asked as they gathered the last pieces of paper up off of the floor.

"Yes . . . yes." Jordan repeated looking into Alec's eyes wondering why he seemed so concerned. With that she continued on to take her class.

On her lunch break Jordan checked her Blackberry messages. There was one from Mark apologizing for the morning and letting her know he had booked them a dinner date so they could spend quality time away from the baby making project. She smiled secretly to herself, he loved her really.

Jordan had also received a message from Nina telling her she had had the biggest shock of her life that morning at work. Nothing exciting ever happened to Nina especially at her work place. Intrigued she question marked the message.

No reply.

Mark had made dinner reservations at ASK for seven o'clock that evening which gave Jordan plenty of time to arrange her classroom for the up and coming term. All the students had long gone so Jordan decided to go to the ladies and take her pregnancy test. Eager to get as much done a possible she placed the test stick in tissue paper on her desk and waited for the result.

Too many times the scenario was to hold it in her hand in the cold toilet cubicle anticipating the, ifs, buts and maybes. Too many times she felt tormented and depressed. The questions would follow, what are we doing wrong? Am I asking for too much? Then the tears would flow long and hard staining her cheeks as well as her heart when it appeared negative. Then the tears wouldn't stop.

Today Jordan decided to take a different approach. If she put it on her desk and became engrossed in her work her mind would become distracted and she would accept the result much more lightly, she hoped. Maybe, just maybe this time, with no doting or yearning the sun might just shine.

Knock! Knock!

Jordan turned to look at the classroom door. Through the glass she saw Alec.

"What are you doing here at this time Alec?" She asked.

"I was in the Library Miss, I have difficulty concentrating at home sometimes, especially with my little brother pestering me to play computer games all the while. I wondered, before I leave if you could help me with this one question?" Alec pleaded.

Jordan looked at Alec. "Sure," she replied.

Alec was a good student. He was an eighteen year old, mixed race boy, with piercing gray eyes and a mass of dark curly hair. His Mother raised him and his little brother alone as their Father was in prison. Therefore Alec experienced lack of encouragement to succeed and do well with his studies. It seemed as though Alec carried the whole bag of beans for his family. He had high aims and aspirations for himself. He confessed to Jordan that he worked hard because he didn't want to be anything like his parents and he aims to be a better example to his little brother and his own kids. That was his motivation.

Jordan made time for her students, not only because it was her job but because she loved her job and she went into teaching for a reason. She believed each generation should out do the previous one and things should get better within the world.

"Oh gosh!" Jordan gasped, "I have to go now Alec, come on."

Alec started laughing at Jordan as she paraded around the classroom frantically. "Do you have a date Miss?"

"Yes," Jordan laughed back, "I actually do, I have to meet my husband for dinner. I thought it was earlier than this, where's the time gone?"

"Thanks for your help Miss I never meant to keep you," Alec said apologetically.

"You are welcome Alec. As long as you are willing, the help is available. I'm glad you take your studies seriously, with that attitude you will achieve the goals you set yourself in life. The hard part is maintaining it."

With that the two gathered up their belongings. Jordan dragged her bag off of her desk knocking the pregnancy test to the floor.

"Miss you dropped something," Alec said bending down to pick it up. Realizing what it was he handed it over to Jordan quickly.

"Thank you," she said as she took the test from Alec's hand reading that it displayed negative.

"Sorry," Alec said.

Jordan looked into Alec's gray eyes.

"For what?" she asked.

"I don't know." He replied truthfully.

With that they both departed.

Jordan got into her Renault Meganne and placed her head in the steering wheel. She felt weird. She didn't know whether she was upset about the pregnancy test showing negative yet again, or if she was slightly embarrassed that Alec witnessed the situation. Whatever it was she couldn't shake it.

She arrived at the restaurant ten minutes late.

"I'm so sorry I'm late babes," she mooched at Mark kissing him on his lips.

"You look flustered, are you ok?" He asked moving the wine glasses around the table to make some space.

"I was just preparing my classroom for the new term and time got away with me," she explained.

"And . . . ?" Mark smirked whilst pouring her a glass of Wine.

Knowing what he was questioning Jordan looked into her glass sadly, "Sorry Mark, not this time."

"We will just have to keep trying then won't we?" Mark assured her with a wink.

2

NINA.

"FOLLOW ME!" THE 'chick' instructed NINA.

Nina contemplated for a moment regretting being hasty. Her lunch break was over and Mr Allen was expecting her to return to work. Then there was the issue of her not wanting the 'chick' to know her place of work as Mr Allen was her client after all.

Think Nina think, she told herself. Her day had been crazy from the start so whilst in the daring and spontaneous mood she decided to call Mr Allen and tell him she was feeling unwell. She did not have a bad sick record if one at all so she was sure he would believe her. It was a little late to turn back now . . . it was now or never, the ball was in her court.

Nina followed the 'chick' to a small quiet café on the Bearwood High street. They sat in a corner by the window. The lunchtime rush was over and the café was calm.

"I'm Claire." The 'chick' introduced herself extending her hand.

"Nina."

They shook hands.

Claire got out her laptop and some papers. Nina looked confused.

"Just to make it look like a business meeting." She informed Nina winking at her to play along. "So what can I do for you?"

"I have seen what you do, purely by accident," Nina started, "Don't get me wrong, I'm not judging you at all, in fact what you do has interested me for a variety of reasons. I want to get into your line of business and I want you to show me how."

Nina went on to explain the attractions. The money, the excitement, the adventure, no routine, a reason to take pride in her appearance and to feel a spark of existence. She watched as a smile slowly spread wide across Claire's face.

Suddenly Nina felt silly as if she had misunderstood, got it all wrong and had made a mistake. She felt as if Claire was making a mockery of her. "What's so funny?" She asked becoming a little nervous.

"You are really serious aren't you?"

"Sure, why wouldn't I be?" Nina retorted, "I have made you come here and dedicate your time, of course I'm serious!"

"OK . . . lower your voice. That's fine, we are clear," Claire confirmed. "Then if that's the case there are so many things we have to run through that will not take just a moment. Also if you are serious this is a business arrangement so I will have to gain from you. I will start you off on a two week trial, show you the ropes help you build up a small clientele of your own until you become established. School you on safety and provide you with awareness tips. Soon after you will be on your own. I'll receive a thirty percent cut off of your first two weeks worth of profit as I will be losing some of mine by working with you during that period. Fair?"

Nina was in awe. What could she say? she never had to ask any questions all was stated loud and clear for her to either take or leave. She liked Claire. The woman was a 'pro player.' She had style, class and pure control. She was a woman who knew what she wanted and no doubt got it. Nina wanted to be at that place and portray that confidence just like Claire.

Claire scoped Nina to see if after hearing the reality of it all she was still in. "People might turn their nose up at what I do but I protect myself and yes I admit I do enjoy it. I work what times suit myself, I'm my own boss and control how much money I earn. Money I do earn because there is a demand for my service. Some women and even men have to question why that does exist. You'll understand what I mean by that when you become familiar with the territory." She finished.

Nina and Claire finished establishing their plans for the next couple of weeks. She knew what she was hoping to gain from this new lifestyle she had so dangerously opted for on the spur of the moment and in her eyes it seemed it was possible to achieve.

Thirty percent is what Claire wanted and Nina was sure to give her that.

Nina turned her key in her front door, kicked off her shoes, pressed her answer machine on and flopped on her couch.

"Nina, it is Mr Allen, just a quick call to check that you are feeling a bit better than earlier today? Let me know when I can expect you back at work. Get well soon."

Nina felt bad for lying, yet at the same time proud of herself for no longer being boring Nina under everybody's thumb. She had taken big risks today, risks the typical Nina would never have ever taken.

What a crazy day.

The clock read 7pm and Nina laughed out loud. She hadn't realized she'd spent so much time with Claire that day.

Munching on a pasta bake she had whipped up in no time, sitting cross legged on her bed surrounded by her faithful cushions listening to the radio, Nina could not help but feel full of butterflies. Decisions had been made that day that were to change her life drastically and as of yet she had no idea if she had done the right thing. Were those butterflies of joy or nerves?

Standing up Nina took off her clothes and admired her body in the full length mirror on her bedroom wall. She smiled as she remembered when she was a little girl her Aunty would say, "If you see something you do not like about yourself in the mirror, look at the things you do like instead and keep on looking at them harder and longer."

She was proud of her body. Compared to other women her age she looked damn good, maybe because she had not yet had any children she thought. But even so, her mother looked incredibly good for her age having had two children. Nina was a nice size ten on top and on the bottom. She had nice shape, not all voluptuous and curvy but she had shape. But one thing bothered her and it was her breasts. They were an average B-cup and pert yes, but she wanted them fuller. "When I've made my first wad of money I'm going to have implants," She promised herself. In her mind she thought it would give her the satisfaction she longed for and boost her clientele within her new lifestyle to come.

Going through her drawers and wardrobe Nina separated her everyday wear from what would be her secret life wear. Knowing it needed revamping she sighed but got all excited at the prospect of renewing it all. She danced around her flat singing along to Ne-Yo's, 'Miss Independent' in her bra and panties laughing to herself.

Ring! Ring!

Nina could barely hear her mobile phone ringing amidst all the music noise. She ran to turn it down and picked up, it was Jordan.

"Hey Jordan, what's up?" She breathed heavily down the phone.

"More like, what are you up to?" Jordan queried, holding the phone slightly away from her ear.

"I was dancing and tidying up my flat that's all." Nina panted.

Jordan wanted to talk. She confided in Nina about how boring the baby making project had become. Nina felt for her especially as it was mostly to satisfy Marks mother. The reasons were all wrong but she wasn't about to state the obvious, Jordan wasn't a fool but she was sensitive. Nina realized how grateful she was for her life as it was, she never had those pressures and right about now she did not crave for responsibility or commitment.

"So what was that crazy thing that happened at work today?" Jordan asked Nina hoping for something juicy.

Nina knew how Jordan assumed her life was boring and full of nothingness. Last Christmas Jordan was drunk and got a bit too merry and told Nina that she needed to do more with her life, get a decent man and have some fun. She practically called her a boring sod! Happy to be going home to her husband and her mortgage and her perfect glittery life Jordan was oblivious of the harm her loose lips had caused to Nina.

"Nothing really," Nina played along, "Mr Allen slipped over at the water machine today flat on his ass and was left with a wet patch." Nina laughed hysterically knowing full well it was not the truth or at all funny but she couldn't tell Jordan the truth as what had really happened that day was the beginning of something new for Nina and she didn't want Jordan to know her secret, this was something to call her own. She was happy for Jordan to continue believing her life was that of a 'boring sods'.

Jordan laughed back half heartedly.

Their conversation soon came to an end after that and Nina cuddled up in her duvet with her pillows, sniffing in the scent of her Lavender sleep spray with the thoughts of the day buzzing around her head like a nest of bees. She was going to have to keep her new life a big secret and play it cool. Cool like Claire.

JORDAN.

"You're my ladeee . . . you're my ladaaeee . . ." Mark sang as he embraced Jordan from behind and swayed to the soft flow of D'Angelo coming through the speakers.

Jordan was seated at the kitchen table marking school papers. Mark started kissing her neck moving up to her ear lobe and then her cheek.

"Baby, please not now I'm busy." Jordan said shrugging Mark off of her.

"Come on its Friday night you have all weekend to do that. Let's go out and have some fun." He laughed, still trying to grab her to dance.

Jordan didn't find him at all funny, he was wrecking her concentration. "God dammit!" She shouted throwing her pen down.

"What have I done?" Mark asked becoming fed up, "I'm trying to show you some love and attention and you keep on pushing me away!"

"Not you baby, I'm sorry I didn't mean to make you feel that way. It's just . . ."

"Just what?" Mark cut her off.

Jordan looked at the name at the top of the paper she was marking, disgusted at the quality of its content.

"One of my star pupils has not turned up for class all week except to hand in an assignment. He never left any explanation for his absence, he didn't look right and his work is not the usual standard. I'm afraid something is wrong," She confessed.

Mark looked long and hard at Jordan and noticed how deeply the situation was affecting her. In his time of teaching he had always noticed how female teachers became more passionate and caring towards their pupils whom they saw great potential and ability in.

"Listen, let's have a nice weekend and go out. You can tackle this issue on Monday, you never know everything might return to normal and he'll come to class. Go up and pick an outfit I'll run you a bath." Mark convinced her.

Jordan ran up the stairs and put 1xtra on the radio to get into the party spirit. Mark smiled as he admired her swaying her hips to Ushers OMG as he passed the bedroom making his way to the bathroom to run her a bath.

They entered club SENSE in the Arcadian centre and headed to the bar.

"What you drinking baby?" Mark asked with a cheesy grin sprawled across his face, knowing full well that she was on the soft drinks as she was the designated driver after loosing the coin toss.

The night was spent dancing and laughing. For the first time in a while Jordan was really having a nice time and was grateful Mark had encouraged her to come out.

Mark had made another journey to the bar leaving Jordan to enjoy the music. Sipping on her juice she watched as a familiar figure strolled into the club and weaved in and out of the crowd followed by a small gang. He then leaned against the bar with the group of young men.

Alec.

She recognized that curly hair and those gray eyes straight away.

Mark returned with drinks.

"Hold on baby I'm just going to the ladies I'll be right back." Jordan said trying to get through the crowd leaving Mark waiting. As she was just about to enter the ladies she felt someone touch her shoulder. She spun around to see Alec towering over her the whites of his eyes red from smoking blaze.

"What's up Jordan?" He asked her with a sly grin on his face pushing his luck playing on her uneasiness. "What? We aren't in school so you aren't Mrs, especially all up in this club." He said disrespectfully looking her up and down as if he was chatting up a young girl.

"I'll see you Monday," Jordan stated abruptly walking away.

"Maybe." He said with a drunken smile. "Oh, and Jordan, are you here with your man? You look so fly tonight."

Jordan ignored him leaving him standing alone. Continuing to the ladies she heard Alec's friends approaching him enquiring as to who she was. She leaned against the cubicle door and closed her eyes. She didn't know what was wrong with her and why she was taking it all to heart. She had always thought Alec to be a respectable young man, never did she ever expect him to behave towards her in that manner. She put it down to alcohol and peer pressure.

Walking back over to Mark she scanned the club for Alec and his crew but they were nowhere in sight.

"What's up babe?" Mark asked her grabbing her waist from behind. "You look like you've just seen a ghost."

"Nothing." She said, trying to enjoy the rest of the night without making it obvious that something was wrong.

It was 4am. Jordan lay her head on her pillow listening to the long, hard drunken snores coming from her husband beside her. She couldn't sleep which left plenty of room for thinking. She thought about her marriage and how unhappy she was. She was sick of Mark criticizing her for taking her work seriously, she was tired of trying to please his mother because he was her only spoilt child and she missed her best friend and having fun with her like they used to. She wondered what Nina had done this Friday night. Probably nothing, she thought, tucked up to her chin by 10pm like a grandma knowing her, she concluded in her own mind.

Really Jordan was envious of Nina. Young, single, independent . . . everything she was yearning to be but didn't want to admit it. 'Maybe I did things to young instead of living a little first,' Jordan thought to herself before eventually falling asleep.

3

NINA.

NINA HAD INFORMED Mr Allen that she had been signed off work for two weeks by her Doctor. He was not very happy about it but could not complain as Nina had a very good attendance record.

"Where are you Nina?" Claire barked down the phone, "punctuality is a must in this line of work!"

It was Saturday and Nina felt rough from the night before. She had had a secret rendezvous with a guy she'd dated a long time ago. She had bumped into him on her way back from the Doctors to pick up her sick note. What was supposed to be an innocent pizza and drink out together turned into a little more when she woke up in his bed that morning at 8am with a banging headache.

"Oh gosh!" She screamed jumping up and swooping her clothes up off the floor. "Sorry I really have to get going," she said stumbling over plates and empty condom wrappers.

Nina had made it home showered and dressed and headed straight to the Merry Hill Mall. Unfortunately everyday was to be a working day for Nina for the next two weeks so she had to get into role as she soon would be without Claire. She still couldn't believe she actually was going through with this.

Nina shuffled as fast as she could through the mall in a pair of skinny jeans and a fitted T-Shirt with her kitten heels clicking along the floor.

Claire was already seated at a table waiting with a coffee for them both.

"Good afternoon." Claire said sarcastically.

"I'm so sorry, finding a parking space is crazy here," Nina apologized.

"Late night huh?" Claire laughed, she wasn't stupid. "Listen early is on time, on time is late. You need time to make that perfect entrance." Claire told Nina. "Drink up girl," she said pulling out a list from her purse, "We have a lot to get through today, we are going to shop until we drop."

"Shop for . . . ?" Nina queried.

"You'll see." Claire smirked.

Claire and Nina paraded the mall buying clothes to start. "Black is what we need. It's classy, professional, sophisticated, complimentary but most of all its sexy!" Claire giggled.

Claire then took Nina to Ann Summers and La Senza in order to boost her lingerie collection. She showed Nina things she would have never thought to purchase, corsets, stockings and suspenders and even crotch-less panties. "If you feel good underneath you ooze confidence and sensuality, then your clothes look and fit good on top," Claire schooled Nina.

After that they then went on to buy sexy, everyday outfits for daytime calls, office type wears, pinafore's, pencil skirts and dresses, fitted suits and low cut tops and blouses, which Nina had enough of.

Evening and night wears after that, LBD's, dinner dresses and then jewellery and accessories.

Last but not least, make-up, perfumes and bags.

"A bag has to have plenty of compartments, compartments are necessary." Claire began. "One is needed for all your contraception, condoms, lubricant, morning after pill etc, as we do not want any accidents. Another for cleanliness, wipes, deodorant and perfume. A pocket for your phone, this has to be a separate phone to your personal one. We will go and get you one when we have finished up here."

The girls literally shopped until they dropped. They went to buy Nina a phone, something simple. "You will need to use speed dial so don't forget to set up the important numbers when you get home." Claire told her.

Nina didn't quite follow. Claire continued noticing the puzzled look on her face. "Emergency numbers in case you are in danger or get attacked. You will also need a bodyguard type friend."

"A bodyguard?" Nina asked surprised.

"Yes. Do you have a big, burly male friend you could call on to come to your rescue ASAP if needed?" Claire asked her.

"Well I do have big, burly male friends but I don't want them all up in my business. I don't want them to know what I'm doing." Nina said slightly alarmed at he need for one.

Claire noticed the fear written all over Nina's face and took the gentle approach. "I do respect that Nina but this line of work is to be taken seriously, especially when it comes to your safety. It isn't all flowers and butterflies, there are times you might find yourself in tricky situations where help is necessary. If you do not know anyone, the best I can offer is one of my bodyguards but you will have to pay him if he gets called out."

Nina decided to accept Claire's offer of one of her guards as she really wanted this whole situation to be a private affair. A very private one at that.

"I'll sort that out for you tonight when we attend Martins cocktail party." Claire confirmed.

Nina wasn't even aware they were going out that night and was a little caught off guard. Again Claire sensed this. "No time to waste we need to get you right."

They stopped for lunch at Pizza Hut. They were both starving. Claire ran through other things with Nina and marked them off the list to ensure they had accomplished everything.

Last but not least was a name for Nina.

"What names do your friends have for you?" Claire asked.

Nina really didn't have pet or nicknames as her name was quite simple.

"A different name is ideal, not only does it keep work separate but it acts as an alter ego. It kind of makes the job a performance, a bit like acting. This makes it easier and more enjoyable. So . . . ?"

"Sunshine." Nina suddenly blurted out.

Claire never asked why she chose that name she was just happy she had thought of one.

"That's cool, I like that. Sunshine it is then."

Nina had chosen Sunshine as her name because she believed this whole new adventure was the sunshine after her rain. It was a new beginning in a sense.

Little did she know she was stepping into murky waters. Water swimming with a whole lot of troubles.

It was 4pm when Claire handed Nina a card.

"Meet me at this address for 8pm." She told Nina pointing to the address on the front of the card. "Stay in your car in the parking lot and text me off your new phone when you arrive and I will come out to meet you. The attire will be a LBD and sexy lingerie and heels. Make sure your bag is equipped with the essentials we discussed today, just in case. At this party we will sort you out some form of protection and maybe one or two clients. But most importantly you'll get a taste of the lifestyle and hopefully have fun."

Nina smiled. She was nervous but excited at the same time. She could do this she assured herself.

"Are you ok with all of this?" Claire asked waiting for a reply of certainty. "If not now is your opportunity to opt out, no one is forcing you. After tonight you will have put your feet in the water and gotten them wet."

"I'm fine about it." Nina confirmed.

"You are doing fine. Remember you have me for two weeks." Claire said winking at Nina.

Nina went on a shoe shopping spree before heading home in preparation for the night ahead. As she drove home she practiced introducing herself by her new name. She couldn't help but laugh at herself, sexy underwear and a whole new wardrobe, this was the most unusual sick note in history, who did she think she was?

Ring! Ring! Ring!

The screen read Jordan. Nina pulled over to answer the phone.

"Hey gurrrl, what's up?"

Nina was greeted by crying and sniffles. "What's up Jordan?" She asked full of concern. She felt bad as she couldn't remember the last time her and Jordan had got together, all they seemed to do was talk on the phone lately.

Jordan informed Nina how Mark had stormed off after an argument. He had become fed up of leading the relationship. He had told her she was always miserable and moaning.

Nina didn't know how to respond. She then realized that Jordan was using the baby making project as an excuse as to why their relationship was under strain. She could sense Jordan wasn't happy a while ago but it was not her place to say. Jordan got married through competition. She had always been the same, had to be the first to do things before anyone else. Get a degree, get married, buy a house etc but only now she was realising it wasn't all roses. Where was it written that was the route of satisfaction? It sure wasn't and Jordan was living proof.

"Can I come over to yours tonight for a girly night?" Jordan asked Nina desperately.

Again Nina felt bad. She had plans obviously but she remembered the times she needed her best friend and due to the 'baby making project' she had to take a back seat. And the back seat she took with no moaning and whining because she understood how much it all meant to Mark and Jordan.

"I'm going out tonight but we could do it tomorrow and have a lazy day together?" Nina tried to compromise.

"You're going out? Where?" Jordan questioned with disappointment as if she was Nina's mother.

"To a dinner party." Nina lied smiling to herself.

"Tomorrow then?" Jordan said and hung up abruptly.

JORDAN.

"Mark it's me, please call me when you get this message."

Jordan had set aside her pride and eventually called Mark begging him to come home. They had had a bust up, a big one at that making Jordan realize what was becoming of her marriage. Maybe Mark was right and she wasn't putting much time and effort into their relationship. She never initiated an evening out or offered weekend proposals. When was the last time she surprised him or did something special? Very rarely did she admit when she was in the wrong and work was her greatest distraction. She really did want a baby but in their own time not to please and gain acceptance from his mother.

She dragged her tear stained face into the bathroom and splashed cold water on it. She hated feeling how she did. Powering up the shower Jordan stepped in and let the water beat down against her back long and hard. She lathered up her flannel with some raspberry shower gel and washed up.

Ring! Ring! She heard the house phone ringing and cursed out. "For goodness sake, trust me to be in the shower!"

Hoping it was maybe Nina and not Mark, she dried off and oiled her body and went into the bedroom to blow dry her hair. The answer machine beeped at her and she listened to the message that had been left. It was Mark dampening her hope of them making up. He told her that he was stopping over at his mother's house until Sunday evening because he needed time to clear his mind.

That was the last straw for Jordan and she broke down into tears yet again. An hour later she found herself in her pyjamas on the sofa with her comfort blanket watching Tyler Perry's, Diary of a mad black woman with a tub of Ben and Jerry's ice cream. She contemplated calling Nina for some support or to help raise her spirits but she remembered that she was out for the night.

4

NINA.

NINA HAD JUMPED the first hurdle of meeting Claire at the venue, she had jumped the second hurdle of introductions and lustful stares and the third hurdle of Claire abandoning her politely to branch out and conquer. Nina could not be mad, she saw it as being thrown in the deep end. What better way to learn how to swim?

Leaning over the balcony of Martins posh hotel penthouse suite and letting the cool breeze sweep over her face, Nina sipped on a virgin cocktail asking herself what she was actually doing there. She did not feel uncomfortable or threatened in the slightest, but she realised how life could change drastically in such a short period of time. Her train of thought was interrupted as she felt a hand touch her gently on her waist. Praying it was not someone she knew she slowly turned around.

"Good evening Miss Lady."

This was her first encounter of the night and remembering the reason why she attended the party she was about to play this right.

"Hello." She said, facing a tall, handsome chocolate brother.

"Frank." He held out his hand and Nina took it gently.

"Sunshine." She smiled.

"That you are and a big ray at that." He charmed as he lowered his lips to kiss the back of her hand.

Nina confidently composed herself noticing how Frank undressed her with his eyes. She cut the sexual tension. "So Frank, what is it you do for a living?"

"I own a restaurant in the Jewellery Quarter." He stated loud and proud.

"Do you specialise in a particular cuisine?" Nina continued to probe, pound signs flashing in her eyes.

"A mix, I like to cater for a majority if possible but I'm open to suggestions." He winked at her.

Nina was impressed. He was educated, successful and black. What she could not work out was why he was at this party looking for the likes of her. Scanning the room she thought the same of everybody present and wondered if they thought the same about her to. She wanted to know much more about him but suddenly remembered what Claire had taught her. "You are not their wife or friend. You are not their counsellor. Do not let them into your personal life and do not enter theirs, strictly sex, time and money."

"Here is my card." Frank handed Nina his business card with his phone number and restaurant address. "How about we make an arrangement for Monday evening at 7pm. You can come and dine with me, sample my cuisine and much more, I'll have you home by midnight, what do you say?" He asked Nina tilting her chin in his hand. "I'll make it well worth your while." He guaranteed her.

"Monday it is then." Nina smiled handing him her card (that Claire had made up for her that same day) before strutting across the room to the ladies. She caught Claire's eye on her way and Claire winked at her proudly having observed discreetly from her corner of the room.

Four hours later with three client cards and two appointments for the following week in toe, Nina entered her flat and unzipped her LBD, kicking off her Miu Miu shoe boots at the same time. She loosened her corset and flopped on her bed falling into slumber land.

Buzzzzzz! Buzzzzzz!

Nina was startled out of her sleep by her doorbell. She jumped up and looked at the clock. It was 2pm Sunday afternoon.

"What the hell? Who could that be?" She panicked looking around at the state of her flat. She had her clothes strewn everywhere and her bag spilled open revealing client cards, pepper spray and plenty more of her new life. She then looked at herself in the mirror and frowned. She scrambled to answer the intercom. "Hello?"

"Nina it is me! I have been out here for ages. I was ringing your phone and getting voice mail, did you forget our date?" Jordan hollered with pure agitation.

Nina buzzed her in.

As Jordan burst in Nina ran around like a mad woman frantically picking up and putting things away so as not to leave any evidence of her secret life.

"I take it you had a good night then?" Jordan laughed looking at Nina spilling out of her loose corset. "A corset huh? Since when do you wear one of those?"

"Since I own a dress that requires one to wear a corset." Nina said in a posh accent laughing. "Get comfy I'm going to scrub up, give me twenty minutes." she told Jordan.

Nina quickly scanned the room for her bag putting it away making sure her work phone was switched off. She jumped into the shower breathing a sigh of relief. That was a close call she thought her heart beating hard against her chest.

"So have you heard from Mark?" Nina asked Jordan as they sat on the sofa surrounded by a mass of junk foods.

"He left me a message." Jordan admitted sadly.

"Saying?"

"He is stopping over his mother's until Sunday."

Nina glared at Jordan. "And you have just accepted that?'

"Well what am I supposed to do?" Jordan raised her voice becoming defensive.

"Go around to his mother's and bring him home." Nina said raising her voice back at her. "How do you know he is not waiting and wanting you to make a move for a change? Make him feel appreciated, show him that you want to be with him. Bring him home where he belongs!"

"How dare you sit there and tell me what to do, when you have no relationship!?" Jordan stabbed at Nina.

"You act like I have never been in a long term relationship before!" Nina fired back. "How do you know I never made the same mistake by not fighting for what I wanted so much but pride got in the way? I don't want to see my best friend make the same mistake I did and let years of hard work and love flutter away. You always get your back up when I'm trying to help what's wrong with you?"

Jordan burst into tears for what was probably the fifth time that weekend.

5

JORDAN.

AFTER COMING TO her senses and listening to Nina's reasoning, Jordan finally approached Mark. She cooked him a candle lit meal and set up an aromatherapy bath followed by a massage with an apology.

"I do really love you Mark and I'm so sorry for everything. I'm scared of being without you." Jordan told him whilst rubbing Lavender oil over his broad shoulders. "I want us to have a family but in our own time."

Mark was happy that Jordan had finally set her pride aside and admitted to her behaviour and understood how it had affected him. He loved his wife and hoped they could continue on a level from there on. He felt spoilt at that moment but he still wanted to make Jordan work a little harder, he wasn't about to make it that easy for her. She had to learn that they were supposed to be a team.

It was Monday and Jordan looked around her class to see if one person in particular had made an effort to attend. To her disappointment Alec had not turned up but she held on to hope assuming he could possibly be late. "He's never late though." She told herself.

Regaining her concentration Jordan took her class and trudged on through the rest of the day.

It was the end of Jordan's working day as she loaded up her car in the campus car park. It was then that she spotted Alec walking across the field outside the gate with his little brother. She admired how Alec lifted his brother up in the air and then placed him onto his back and then ran really fast pretending to be a horse. She smiled to herself as Alec's brother giggled all the while clinging on to Alec's sweater for dear life.

Jordan suddenly snapped out of her trance questioning why Alec had not attended class if he was out and about. She decided to go to the head teacher's office to voice her concern.

"How may I help you today Mrs Cunningham?"

Jordan informed the head teacher of Alec's absence and how it seemed odd considering the high standard of work he produced and how enthusiastic he normally was when it came to his studies.

The head teacher sat and listened to Jordan. Jordan had a good reputation and was renowned as a very good teacher. Her students always spoke highly of her and they achieved plausible grades. Jordan was granted permission to do a home visit to try to get to the bottom of Alec's absence.

"You have to remember he is eighteen years of age and is entitled to make decisions of his own so do not approach him all guns blazing demanding him to come back and study, he is a young adult." Were the head teacher's last words.

With that clearly understood Jordan prepared to visit Alec the next afternoon.

"Mark! Are you home?" Jordan shouted wondering around the house, dropping her keys on the coffee table and dumping her bag by the staircase. With no response of any kind she felt a little disheartened. They had just sorted things out between them and she was longing for his embrace. She hoped he wasn't still upset with her.

The answer machine beeped at her and she pressed play. "Hey baby, it's me. I've gone out with a few people from work for a meal, I'll be back later. Don't wait up."

Like a child Jordan stomped upstairs and slumped on her bed with the cold, empty lonely house for company that evening.

It was not until 11pm when Mark arrived home, Jordan pretended to be asleep. "Wake up baby." He whispered loudly into her ear offending her with his garlic breath.

"Ewwww! Baby! Leave me alone you smell!" Jordan laughed trying to roll and twist herself free from him as he climbed on top of her pinning her down, trying to kiss her. Jordan giggled as Mark played around. It was nice to see him smile.

At breakfast the next morning Jordan explained to Mark the situation with Alec and how she had been granted permission to carry out a home visit. "Just be careful and keep it professional," Mark warned her, "The head teacher is right, Alec is eighteen years of age and can make his own decisions. I hope you know what you are doing?"

Jordan looked at Mark a little hurt at his response as if he doubted her competency.

"I do." She replied.

Mark could see she was a little fragile after his comment and felt a little bad. He kissed her forehead and left for work.

NINA.

Nina was still on her sick note and glad for it. She had had a very busy weekend with the added stress of helping Jordan mend things with Mark. She decided to stay in bed for the first time ever on a Monday morning and watch Jeremy Kyle and other morning TV shows that she never had the opportunity to watch with her breakfast in bed. She then planned to have a pamper in order to be at her best for her 7pm appointment with Frank.

"Strictly time, sex and money." She kept reminding herself over again.

Opening her closet doors she became stuck for what to wear, she was spoilt for choice. "If you feel good underneath you ooze sexiness and sensuality." She heard Claire's voice. Nina decided on her lacy wonder bra with matching thong. She picked a low cut Benetton dinner dress with her Vivian Westwood peep toe stilettos, white gold bracelet and earrings and minimal make-up but scarlet red lips.

Walking up and down her hallway spraying her Prada Milano perfume and letting it settle upon her, she gazed at herself in the mirror. She felt nervous as she looked at herself. She looked and felt like a totally different woman.

"I can do this." She told herself. "Hello Sunshine."

Nina was supposed to meet Frank at his restaurant for 7pm. She decided to take a taxi as alcohol would definitely be essential to get her through the night ahead plus she didn't want him to know what car she drove.

It was 6:30pm and Nina's work phone beeped as she applied her finishing touches. It was Frank reminding her that he was expecting her and not to be late.

As Nina entered the restaurant all eyes were on her as Frank greeted her at the door and escorted her to her seat at a centre table. A well presented waiter approached them handing them menus. He then took their beverage orders smiling all the while.

"Why is everyone watching and smiling?" Nina asked Frank starting to feel a little uncomfortable. She felt as if she was on display at a museum.

"Because you look gorgeous and as the owner of this place the staff are on their best behaviour in order to impress me." He said trying to make her feel more at ease.

As the two dined together Frank could not help but admire how nice and sexy Nina looked. He could tell she was a lady of class and high standards. He could imagine she had to have the best of everything and that's what had drawn him to her initially. He licked his lips as he caught sight of her defined collar bone and her soft, succulent red lips.

They became engrossed in meaningless conversation and two hours later Frank had them chauffeured off to the Ramada hotel in the Mailbox plaza. He had a Penthouse suite set up for them with champagne, strawberries and cream and a Jacuzzi. Nina scanned the room trying to tame the butterflies raging inside of her stomach. "I can do this." she said silently.

"Sunshine, I'm going to get well adjusted in the Jacuzzi," Frank whispered into Nina's ear as he nibbled on her earlobe taking in the scent of her perfume. "Why don't you come and join me and show me what sexy lingerie you have hugging that sexy body of yours." he coaxed her. On the way to the Jacuzzi Frank hit the power button on the stereo and the soft voice of Joe filled the room. "Don't be shy, you're beautiful, I promised I would make it worth your while and I stick to my word."

Nina composed herself and clicked into 'Sunshine' mode. She seductively strolled slowly toward Frank casually stepping out of her dress and letting it fall to the floor revealing nothing but her underwear. Frank climbed into the tub, ushering for Nina to join him. She left her heels at the side of the tub and climbed in towering above him as he sat looking up at her body. He rubbed his hands up her smooth legs reaching her thighs. Cherishing every inch of her body he placed cream on the inside of her thighs and licked it off, his warm, moist tongue causing Nina to moan. He tugged at her thong and so she stepped out of it. He then pulled her lower to him so she could straddle him in the Jacuzzi bubbles. He unclipped her bra filling his mouth with her breasts sucking on her nipples with ice cubes in his mouth amazed at how erect they became. Nina moaned . . . why did this feel so good? Nina felt his nature rise and reached over to the side for the condoms.

Nina rolled over and peeped her watch with one eye, it was 11:45pm. Frank was worn out and Nina was ready to go home and shower. She started gathering her stuff together and went into the bathroom to freshen up for the journey home.

"That was amazing." Frank said kissing Nina's shoulder and neck. She moved him off of her shyly and told him her taxi was waiting outside. He handed her an envelope. "How about Friday night at 10pm?" he asked her. "I'll meet you here in this exact same room and I would love for you to spend the whole night until midday check out time Saturday. What do you say?"

"I'll let you know by Wednesday." Nina replied nonchalantly. She did not want to seem keen and she wanted him to also think she was in demand although he was her first client she didn't want him to know that. She intended on making money. She was curious as to how much was in the envelope he had handed her but planned on opening it in the taxi ride home.

"I'll be waiting for your confirmation then." Frank said holding Nina's stare.

With that Nina left the suite and got into her taxi.

Once inside the taxi and halfway home Nina opened the envelope Frank had given her to find a cheque enclosed for one thousand pounds. Her jaw dropped. Not bad for a few hours, she smiled to herself full of awe and glee.

Lying in her bed that night, Nina wondered why anyone would pay an extortionate amount of money for what she had done with Frank that night. Wouldn't it be easier to find a stable partner to love and care for and share many experiences together at the cost of love?

She wasn't complaining her pockets were fat and she had enjoyed being wined and dined as well as the luxury of the plush hotel suite. She even enjoyed the sex, it all seemed too easy. What she had made in one night would take her two weeks or more to make at Mr Allen's.

Nina's work phone beeped. It was a voice message from Frank. "I hope I showed my gratitude enough. There is plenty more where that came from. I'll be awaiting confirmation for Friday."

Just business Nina reassured herself.

"Goodnight Sunshine." She laughed out loud.

6

JORDAN.

Ding dong! Ding dong!

Jordan stood outside Alec's house ringing the bell anticipating his reaction when he opened the door and saw her standing there. She heard scuffling noises and banging as she waited nervously. Checking the time on her DKNY watch which Mark had purchased for her birthday last year she made it just past 1pm and she was on her lunch break and starving. "Come on Alec." She said out loud tapping her foot becoming impatient. Someone was clearly inside the house she could hear them.

Finally the door swung opened and Alec glared at Jordan long and hard. No longer were his eyes gentle and gray they were sharp and piercing. "What are you doing here?" He questioned her with sheer disapproval.

"Listen, Alec . . . I got permission from the head teacher at school. I'm not here to cause trouble I just want to see if you require any help and I want to know why you haven't been attending my class." Jordan spurted out as quickly as she possibly could afraid he was going to slam the door in her face before hearing her out.

It was apparent Alec was angry.

"Can I come in and talk to you?" She asked, not wanting to stand on his doorstep and hold a conversation for the neighbours to hear.

Jordan noticed Alec constantly observing his surroundings and looking over his shoulder into the house.

"No you can't Miss. There is nothing to talk about. I have decided to drop out of college and that's it." He said it as if he was sure of himself. "Just accept it and leave me alone.' He warned her.

"I know that's not the truth Alec." With that Jordan turned and started down the path to her car. As she proceeded she heard shouting coming from inside Alec's house.

"Alec? Who was that at my front door? Huh?"

Jordan presumed it to be his mother and was quite astonished at the atrocious language but she bit her tongue and carried on to her car. The shouting continued as Alec closed the door, "What does she want? Tell her to mind her own business the nosey cow!"

Sitting in her car Jordan contemplated returning to Alec's door but changed her mind quite quickly, she knew her place. She knew something was wrong she felt it. Alec confided in her, told her his dreams and ambitions. The person he had become lately just wasn't him. It wasn't her hardworking, well mannered student.

On her way back to work Jordan stopped off at the corner store not far from Alec's house to get a chocolate fix. As she walked out of the shop Alec walked in.

"Why can't you just leave me alone?!" He snapped.

Jordan just walked on and ignored him, she didn't want confrontation in the local shop, not her style and definitely not up to embarrass herself so she ignored him and walked on noticing the basket full of cleaning products Alec was about to purchase.

Tap! Tap! Tap! Sitting inside of her car, Jordan looked up with a mouthful of chocolate to find Alec banging on her drivers side window with sad puppy dog eyes.

She wiped her mouth, "Alec?" She questioned, caught off guard, winding her window down.

"I'm sorry, can I meet you at the 'Tree' in ten minutes?" He pleaded.

"Sure, ok."

41

Jordan saw the sadness in his eyes and felt as if she'd pressured him into talking to her. Had she made him feel guilty by not reacting to his bad attitude? All she cared about was getting to the bottom of whatever was happening so he could get on with his life with the necessary help. She sensed it was a domestic problem from his mother's foul mouth and the amount of cleaning products Alec had just bought, even watching him play with his brother the other day. Why should the younger ones be responsible for where their parents were failing? Why should they be deprived of opportunities and privileges having to pick up where their parents gave up?

Jordan sat on the bench underneath the 'Tree' in Kingsheath Park. It was called the 'Tree' as it was the largest weeping willow. It was the place of peace and to air troubles.

She kept looking around hoping Alec wasn't messing her around. It had been fifteen minutes and Jordan was getting ready to leave. Just as she gave up hope Alec appeared up the path with his hood up and his hands stuffed deeply inside of his pockets. He sat down beside her and pulled his hood off his head ruffling up his curly hair. Jordan remained quiet she didn't want to say the wrong thing and cause Alec to scarper so she left the ball in his court. He glanced at her sideways and fidgeted.

"You are right Miss. I never wanted to stop coming to class. I want to go to University and make something of myself but right about now I just ..."

Jordan waited for him to continue, it was killing her not being able to encourage the conversation.

"It's my mum." He hung his head low as tears dropped out of his eyes and fell like raindrops landing on his jeans.

Jordan dug into her bag and found a handy pack of tissues. She handed him one which he accepted and scrunched up in his hand defeating its purpose.

"My mum is taking drugs and she is addicted. She's not fit to look after our home or my little brother who's only eight years old. She's a wreck and she can't stop so I have to do it all. I've had to pack in my studies to sort this out Miss. I'm scared! I don't want my brother taken away so I didn't tell you because I was scared you'd call social services. What am I supposed to do? I will fix this and get back to my studies but my brother is just a kid he needs me!"

Jordan tried to swallow back all the emotion. The sight of this young boy breaking down was unfair.

"Listen Alec we will sort this as best as we can. I'll get you some numbers to call or we'll call them together to get your mom some help first . . ."

"NO!" Alec shouted cutting her off. "I shouldn't have told you, this was a mistake!"

Alec got up and pulled his hood up over his head and marched off.

"Alec, wait!" Jordan got up and ran after him. "Don't do this we have to sort this out, you can't go on like this. This isn't just about your studies, it's more than that. This will remain confidential between you and me, I promise!" As soon as those words left her lips she knew they shouldn't have and it was too late to take them back.

Alec slowed down and turned to look at Jordan. "Help me miss." He begged pleading silently at her with his big, sad, gray eyes.

"I'll do my best Alec. You do what you need to do at home and I'll gather some help and information to help sort out the drug addiction with your mom as I told you. You can tell her that you got the information and you are sorting it yourself if that makes it easier. When you are ready we'll sort out your studies I could drop off your work or you could come to class and pick it up whatever is convenient for you. At least if we get you through these exams you could then have a gap year before going to University to ensure all is well at home. But home is what we need to concentrate on first and the wellbeing of your brother and mother. It will be tough Alec but it will sort."

Jordan got back to work unable to concentrate and feeling sad. She hated seeing Alec in such a state and she so badly wanted to hold him tightly and bat all his problems away.

She text Nina to ask her to meet up for a drink and dinner at New Sum Ye that evening, she needed to vent. Unfortunately Nina was not responding and Jordan took the pressure of her day home with her. She felt as if she couldn't speak to Mark after what he had said to her that morning but she had also promised Alec confidentiality. She had to pretend that Alec had just decided to drop out of college,

NINA.

Nina's sick note was coming to an end. She could hardly believe all the things she had become involved in enduring her new lifestyle as an Escort. Character swapping was now second nature to her as well as picking the appropriate attire for certain clients and occasions. Speaking of clientele, she had built up quite a good one in such a short period of time and had had at least one encounter with each of them. She had to keep tabs on the amount of clients she was going to have as she was still going to remain in legit part time employment and needed to consider the time she could afford to dedicate to each of them.

Frank seemed to be the most popular and demanding out of the lot so far but she wasn't complaining because the treatment she received off him was excellent and he paid her well, very well indeed. Admittedly she even enjoyed the company and the sex with him. All she had to be was 'Sunshine' and he'd pull out all the stops!

There was a Limo driver by the name of Ryan who had this fetish for her to have sex with him after he had finished a night shift. He liked it in the back of the Limo with her on top in her crotch less panties and heels. As weird as it seemed she just thought about the money.

Another one of her clients liked her to sit on his face while he satisfied her lady world, no penetration, he would just bust a nut all over himself and that was satisfaction enough for him Again, no complaints, just payment.

She had a client who reminded her of Mr Allen in the sense that he liked raunchy office sex. This guy would hoist her up the office door, place her on top of the photo copy machine or the desk top and he liked it doggy style up the window on the 11th floor for the world to see! At the end of the heated performance she would have blouse buttons missing, breasts spilling out and tousled hair.

What Nina never understood was why she never felt dirty or ashamed. Why did she enjoy it? It wasn't easy but it was easy to enjoy once she got into character. It was exciting but hard maintaining it a secret. She constantly had to be aware and careful so as not to let the slightest things slip. She didn't want any of her clients knowing where she lived or what car she drove and so taxi was the best form of transport.

She did contemplate packing in her job fully because the money she was making as an Escort was fantastic, but that would be too risky to soon. She had to have some constancy in her life so as not to raise suspicion, it was early days, very early day's, right about now she hadn't even started walking properly yet.

"I'm just getting a little bit ahead of myself." She assured herself, "calm down Nina, calm down."

It was Friday and Nina was up and showering. She lathered the cocoa butter body wash all over her body touching herself and smiling as she thought of Franks lips kissing her inner thighs. Just as she stepped out the shower her work phone rang. She answered in her most seductive voice. "Hello."

"Sunshine, its Frank."

"Hiya Frank, and what can I do you for?" She laughed quietly to herself.

"I need you today in my office at my restaurant. It's quite urgent. I have had a terrible day and I need some comfort. What do you say?"

"What time?" Nina asked knowing she had an appointment to keep with Claire at 1pm.

"Lunchtime." was the dreaded answer.

Nina wanted this fat cheque and tried to compromise. "How about 3pm as I have to meet my girlfriend at 1pm?"

"That will be fine then . . . oh, please wear that red lipstick I like." He requested.

Nina parked her car in Star City and met Claire in Nando's. For once Nina was there before her by a minute or two. Claire pulled up a seat and smiled. "Early is on time and on time is late!" They both laughed in unison, smelling the tantalising aroma of the chicken being barbequed on the hot grill.

"Well Little Miss Sunshine, this is farewell I guess." Claire began.

Nina dug into one of the compartments of her bag and pulled out an envelope and handed it to Claire. "Here is your thirty percent, as promised." Nina said proudly.

Claire smiled and took the envelope.

"So how has it been for you so far? Any problems? Any sweaty, smelly willies to suck? Fat, ugly men to shag?" She giggled like an immature teenager.

Nina made a wretching sound as if she were vomiting. 'Not yet but I know it'll come."

"Remember you are your own boss." Claire told her as they finished their lunch. Claire had to get back to her full time demands but she reassured Nina she would be there for her if ever she did need her, she was just a phone call away.

Nina thanked her gratefully for all of the time and guidance she had provided. She would always hear Claire's voice in her head with warnings and lessons. Claire had helped her step into a new life. Not what the average person may have wanted or even considered, but it suited Nina just fine and for once she was smiling. She felt confident and outgoing, a new woman. She now felt alive.

"Remember do not mix your personal life with work." Were Claire's lasts words as her and Nina went their separate ways.

Nina checked her Guess watch it was 2pm. She went to the ladies and fixed herself up ready for Frank. Once inside her car she applied her scarlet Dior lipstick (as requested) and sprayed on her Prada perfume.

Due to time she had to go straight to Franks so she drove to the Jewellery Quarter and parked a couple streets down walking the rest of the way.

"Excuse me I have an appointment to see Frank at 3pm." Nina told the busy bartender.

"Who shall I say is here?" He asked looking her up and down lustfully, grinning.

"Sunshine.' She answered holding his gaze.

He disappeared and when he returned he asked her to climb up a couple flights of stairs to Franks office. Nina was aware that the bartender was checking out her legs and trying to peek up her skirt so on purpose she switched her hips dramatically from side to side.

"Thank you." Nina said as he showed her to Frank's office door. Nina did the final checks to her attire before knocking the door.

"Come in." Frank summoned.

Nina slowly opened the door and entered. Frank stood up from his desk and walked over to her. He locked the door behind her and grabbed her wrist gently, pulling her into him and kissing her lightly on her cheek.

"Looking good enough to eat as usual." He complimented her.

He started to undo her shirt buttons and planted kisses down her neck and on her collar bone tracing his fingers to her breasts.

"What happened today to make you upset then?" Nina asked adjusting to her role.

"It doesn't matter now that you are here." He said lifting her up and carrying her over to the office couch. He lay her down gently and hungrily licked her breasts, sucking on her nipples. He then worked his way down towards her belly button continuing further removing her French knickers invading her private area. Nina felt so much pleasure she whimpered craving him to continue. Frank took off his clothes and pulled Nina on top of him. She placed a condom on his extremely erect penis and lowered herself down his pole.

All cleaned up and ready to leave Nina noticed it was 5pm on the wall clock. They had been at it for two hours. As usual Frank handed her an envelope and smiled feeling refreshed after being released from sexual tension.

"Before you go Sunshine may I ask you a question?"

"Go ahead?" Nina looked puzzled.

"How do you feel when you spend time with me?"

Claire's voice echoed in her head. 'You are not their wife, friend or counsellor.'

"It's a job Frank." Nina told him straight gathering up her belongings to leave.

"Well I like you a lot and I don't like the thought of you being with . . ." He let it hang. "You are right. I'm out of order, it doesn't matter."

With that Nina left Franks office leaving her silence behind.

Nina got home and ran a nice hot bath with candles and oils. She put her India Arie album on and sunk into the water closing her eyes. She was due back at work on Monday and had to go through the process of convincing Mr Allen to give her part time hours. She was no longer prepared to commit and dedicate herself to a full time job she found no fulfilment in anymore.

Her mind then ran on Frank. It had only been two weeks and three encounters and already he was getting emotionally attached to her. It was becoming intense and she began questioning if she had done anything to encourage him to behave that way. From the get go the arrangement was clear as crystal.

She put her head beneath the water drowning out the sounds and blew bubbles.

All tucked up in bed in her PJ's and a cheese salad sandwich Nina called Jordan to catch up. She felt bad as she had let her down earlier on in the week for a dinner date. Jordan had sounded real upset on the voice message to but Nina was tied up in her secret life.

"What's up girl?" Nina asked Jordan whilst brushing the bread crumbs off of her chest.

"I'm fine Nina. Long time, what have you been up to?"

Jordan didn't sound right.

"I'm ok."

"It's just that I popped into your work place today as a surprise to grab some lunch to make up for us not being able to get a dinner date the other night and you weren't there. Mr Allen told me you have been off work for two weeks sick and you are due back Monday. Is that right?"

Nina's heart started beating double time. Since when did Jordan surprise her for lunch? "Yes that's right." Nina confessed.

"Well I then paid a visit to your flat to see if I could help out in any way and to see if you were ok but again you weren't there either. Is everything ok Nina? What's going on? You haven't been around lately."

Nina had to think and fast. She had to cover this up convincingly. "I popped out to the supermarket to get some fresh air and a few bits and bobs. I was signed off by the Dr with stress," Nina lied, "but yes, I am back at work on Monday."

"Why didn't you tell me?"

"You had a lot of stuff going on and I didn't want you stressing out. I don't even know if I was stressed, that's just what the Dr said. Anyway stress or not, the break off work did me good and I'm going to be fine to get back to work on Monday. I'm sorry I have been distant and I didn't tell you. We'll make it up. Let's go out tomorrow night and party. What do you say?"

Jordan agreed easily, desperate for a change of scenery, and so it was settled.

Nina was just about to lay her head down to sleep when she received a text on her work phone. It was Frank. 'Sunday dinner?'

Nina laughed, it seemed like he liked to spend money and time on her. She knew she would have to call Claire and get some sound advice on how to handle Frank. She would do it tomorrow she was tired. Closing her eyes Nina realized she had to be more careful, keeping this life a secret was becoming hard especially from Jordan.

7

JORDAN.

JORDAN CLIMBED OUT of bed and wondered downstairs into the kitchen where Mark was cooking scrambled eggs and toast whilst dancing to 1xtra in his boxer shorts. She leaned against the door frame watching him trying to stifle her laughter. It was when he reached for the wooden spoon to act as his microphone that Jordan couldn't contain her laughter anymore and let it loose bringing attention to her presence. Mark spun around startled and embarrassed stubbing his big toe on the corner of the table.

"Baby that is not funny!" He whimpered as he grabbed a chair to sit down and rub his toe.

"Aww, you poor baby." Jordan purred at him trying to make him feel better.

Jordan straddled him and he embraced her with hugs and kisses. Things had just resumed to normal between them, the silly games they played like teenagers in love, dining at home together as well as the affection they showed each other.

"What are we doing today?" Mark asked Jordan knowing full well what the answer was going to be.

"I thought we could go shopping together." She laughed.

"Shopping for you is what you mean." He corrected her making her aware he knew her tricks,

"Well I'm going out tonight with Nina so I'm in need of a new frock." Jordan justified.

Mark screwed up his face before eventually agreeing to be dragged around town.

Mark and Jordan wondered the Bullring stacking up bargains whilst enjoying each other's company. Jordan had purchased a black, sharp edge cut dress from Vero Moda and Mark had treated her to not one, but two new pairs of shoes, a classy pair from Kurt Geiger and a funky pair from Office. Surprisingly he let Jordan buy him a DKNY shirt and a pair of Diesel jeans. They had lunch at the Sushi bar in Selfridges before heading back to the car.

Whilst driving out of the city centre they stopped at a set of traffic lights by the Radisson hotel.

"Hey baby, isn't that Nina?" Mark asked pointing across to the hotel where a lady stepped out of a taxi in a LBD looking smart yet sexy.

Squinting her eyes Jordan tried to make her out. "It is her, but what is she doing going in there today, at this time and dressed like that?" She questioned all at once as if Mark knew the answers.

"Shall I honk the horn?" Mark asked with his hand hovering over the horn ready.

"No!" Jordan snapped.

The lights changed to green and they carried on home.

"She looked good though." Mark commented with a big grin on his face.

"Hey that's my girl!" Jordan slapped his shoulder getting her back up.

"I was just saying." He laughed.

Once back home Jordan snuggled up to Mark for a late afternoon nap. Whilst drifting off her mind ran on Nina. Something seemed odd but she couldn't figure it out. She had been acting weird lately. The times Jordan needed her she was unavailable whereas before she used to be quite reliable. Then there was the sick note secret and when they had a lazy day date and her flat was a mess with clothes strewn everywhere from her sudden social life. The other thing Jordan questioned was the type of clothes Nina was wearing for example the corset and LBD's?

Jordan's mind continued to run. It ran on Alec as she wondered what his Saturday had entailed, the poor thing. She dreaded to imagine what he had to contend with at home, cleaning up for his mother whilst she shouted abuse after him and then having to soothe his little brother with lies and pretence.

Eventually sleep came over her as she rested her cheek underneath Marks prickly chin.

NINA.

Nina hailed a black cab and headed home. She had just finished with a client at the Radisson hotel and made a nice profit. She had just enough time to get herself ready for her night out with Jordan. Nina decided that tonight she was going to really have a good time as she was back at her mundane nine to five job on Monday morning her sick note required a farewell to remember.

"Thanks mate keep the change." Nina generously added as she stepped out of the cab rummaging into the depths of her Marc Jacobs handbag for her apartment keys.

Her personal phone beeped, it was a text message from Jordan reminding her to be on time. At times Nina had to laugh to herself at the typical teacher Jordan was.

Nina quickly put an outfit together, she was out to impress and turn heads tonight. She opted for her backless, black, short fitted dress with her Mango, open toe shoe boots. As she hung her dress on her closet door and was just about to step into the shower, her work phone rang out.

"Hello?" Nina said hurriedly.

"It's me, Frank."

"Frank I'm sorry but I'm off duty tonight."

"Oh . . ." Frank moaned disheartened. "How about tomorrow for Sunday lunch then?" He asked in hope.

"Ok Frank, tomorrow for lunch, I have to go I'm in a bit of a rush." And with that Nina hung up, turned off her work phone and finished getting ready.

Nina and Jordan got out of the taxi outside club Boujee on Broad Street. It was midnight as they entered the club bouncing to Fifty Cent and Ne-Yo's, 'Baby by me.'

"Right, what are you drinking?" Nina asked Jordan as they shuffled their way through the crowded bar.

"Errmmm . . ." Jordan tried to decide her poison as she scanned the contents behind the bar spoilt for choice, not used to being able to drink as she was always the designated driver.

"How about some Pink Champagne?" Nina said and before Jordan could agree or not Nina had an iced bucket of Champagne in her arms and they were waltzing over to a corner booth.

"What's the occasion?" Jordan shouted to Nina over the music.

"No occasion." Nina smiled pouring each of them more than a glass full. "We haven't done this in a while so lets do it properly."

Jordan sipped some of her Champagne peering at Nina over the rim of her glass. "I'm not just talking about the drink but your dress to, it's a bit revealing for you isn't it? Not to mention you splashing the cash hey?"

"I don't know what you mean?" Nina said beginning to wonder what Jordan was trying to get at.

"It doesn't matter. I'm a little stressed with an issue at work and I shouldn't have brought it out with me. I apologise. Go and hit the floor like you usually do." Jordan encouraged Nina whilst pouring herself another glass of Champagne. At least she could drink some of her stresses away tonight.

Nina loved to dance. She loved to move to every beat of a tune. Music seemed to take over her and send her into her own little world especially if she was a little tipsy to.

Jordan watched Nina from the booth with a hint of jealousy. Nina was dressed to impress and not just tonight but every time she had seen her of late. Not only that but she seemed much more confident in herself and so busy all the time. Jordan felt left out as if she was missing something, but she was curious as to what it was she was missing.

Nina was in her element, she scanned the club and caught Jordan's eyes ushering her to come over and dance with her to Ne-yo's 'Closer' their favourite song. Jordan refused with a plastic smile. She just wasn't in the mood.

Nina made her way back to the bar to purchase a bottle of white wine to add to their drinks collection

"Slow down!" Jordan snapped at Nina.

"Ok grandma!" Nina giggled but Jordan didn't find her amusing.

Nina went back to the dance floor. Jordan was ruining her farewell sick note night and she was not happy. She didn't understand what she was supposed to have done in order for Jordan to behave how she was. "Pah!" She spat strutting her stuff.

All of a sudden Nina felt a presence behind her. She turned around slowly to face a very handsome guy, about six foot, olive complexion and hazel eyes. Gorgeous she thought to herself smiling, still dancing along with him to the music. He placed his hands around her waist as they swayed in unison and he whispered in her ear, "You are really nice, I noticed you from the other side of the club you seem so content, I love how you move your body to the music. I hope you don't mind but I just had to come and dance with you."

Nina smiled, he smelt so sweet.

"My name is Aaron." He introduced himself spinning her around to face him.

"Sun . . . erm . . . Nina." She said caught off guard, nearly slipping forgetting she was off duty and this was her personal, recreational time.

"Nina?" He asked verifying her name.

"Yes, that's correct."

At that moment Jordan approached them. Nina was just about to politely carry out introductions when Jordan said she was leaving.

"Excuse me one moment please." Nina told Aaron as she dragged Jordan over to the booth. "Why are you leaving?" She asked all confused by Jordan's attitude throughout the entire night. "It's only 1am?"

"I'll be ok. I'll jump in a cab and text you when I reach home. You go and have some fun with that guy, I haven't seen you smile like this in a while and I feel like I'm ruining the vibe with my miserable self." Jordan admitted.

Nina didn't know whether Jordan was passing a compliment or being patronising. "Ok, whatever you want to do." Nina started making her way back over to the dance floor.

Jordan grabbed her arm sternly, "Nina, be safe and text me when you get home."

Nina watched as Jordan exited the club. Really she wanted to ask her what the problem was and what was going on with her lately but it wasn't the time or the place. Not prepared to have her night spoilt Nina resided in the booth and drank a glass of wine straight off angry that she had been abandoned by her best friend.

"Are you ok?" Aaron asked sliding into the booth next to her.

Nina looked at him and smiled. "Yes," she reassured him, "My friend just left, she isn't feeling to good."

"Well, can I get you another drink?" He asked.

"No thanks I've had enough."

"Let's dance then." Aaron offered her his hand. Nina took it and they hit the dance floor.

Nina had a fantastic night with Aaron. They danced and laughed together as if it was just the two of them in the club. They left at 3am and went to the Chippy and shared a portion of chips with mayonnaise.

"So do you always come out on your own?" Nina slurred at Aaron dipping her chip into some mayo.

Aaron laughed, "I never came out on my own intentionally. I was supposed to meet my friend at the club but he let me down so I decided to chill on my own. I'm glad I chose to as well." He smiled and winked at her.

They both shared a cab home, Aaron insisted he make sure Nina got home safely.

Nina removed her shoes once inside the cab and Aaron scooped up her feet and placed them on his lap. "Feet hurting?" He asked rubbing them gently whilst watching Nina enjoying his touch.

Nina purred with pure delight. She couldn't remember the last time, if any, when a man had rubbed her feet let alone gave her such a good night out. She didn't care that Jordan had branched out on her, in fact she didn't care about much at that precise moment. She was merry.

The cab pulled up outside of her flat and she got her belongings together. She took a ten pound note out of her purse for her share of the cab fare but Aaron refused it. "I'll get the fare, let me walk you to your door."

"Ok." Nina said carefully stepping out of the cab shoes dangling in her hands.

"I won't be a moment," Aaron told the driver as he admired how Nina swaggered up the path eventually making it to the door.

"Listen Nina, I know you're a little tipsy but I really like you," he told her, "and I'd really like to see you again. What do you say? Can we exchange numbers?"

Nina was flattered and Aaron was right she was tipsy as the digits to her personal phone rolled freely off her tongue. Aaron got real close to Nina and kissed her cheek, "Goodnight sexy lady." He made his way back to the cab walking backwards, hands in his pockets admiring her and smiling.

Nina let herself into her flat and flopped on her bed falling into a deep, drunken sleep.

8

JORDAN.

"You got home quite early last night, did you have a good time?" Mark asked Jordan the next morning as she brushed her teeth in the bathroom mirror.

Jordan spat her toothpaste into the sink, "Yes, we had a great time." She lied trying to hide the fact that she was the greatest disappointment to Nina let alone herself. "It was fun I just didn't want to stay out to late because we have dinner at your mothers this afternoon and you know how she can be at the slightest detection of one using precious baby making time to gallivant."

Mark stared at Jordan trying not to respond to her spiteful comment regarding his mother. Why was she making personal digs? Or was Jordan simply in one of her bad moods? Deciding not to entertain her, knowing it would lead to an argument, Mark let it slide and left Jordan in the bathroom whilst he made his way downstairs to the kitchen to make a cup of coffee. He decided against breakfast as he didn't want to spoil his appetite for his mothers great Sunday feast.

Jordan remained in front of the bathroom mirror dabbing the toothpaste from around her mouth. She still hadn't received a text off Nina confirming she had made it home safely last night. Did she even make it home last night? Jordan wondered not putting anything past Nina of late, due to the changes she had noticed in her.

Jordan's stomach became tight as they neared Marks mothers house in Walsall. She hated visiting her knowing exactly the order in which things would play out. At the front door Mark would be greeted first with big hugs and smooching kisses. Jordan would receive an air kiss filled with nothingness and then she would be checked out from head to toe and back up again to ensure one, she was suitably dressed and two, if she had gained any weight. Baby weight. If no baby weight was present Jordan would have to put up with her smart mouth remarks for the duration of the visit.

The dread was setting in so deep it hit the pit of Jordan's stomach as they pulled up on Marks mother's drive.

"Smile baby, mom cannot wait to see you." Mark said kissing her cheek trying to ease her tension.

"More like to see if I'm pregnant or not!" Jordan snapped clambering carefully out of the car so as not to tread on any of the perfectly groomed flowers bordering the driveway.

Marks mother opened the front door and all unfolded just as Jordan had predicted. It was going to be a very long Sunday afternoon.

It was 8pm before Jordan and Mark were finally freed from the reigns of Marks mother.

"Can we pass by Nina's on the way home?" Jordan asked Mark. "I just want to run in and drop her something that she left with me last night." She said inventing a reason to pass by and be nosey as well as make sure Nina was safe.

As Mark drove to Nina's, Jordan text her to let her know she was passing for a few minutes but got no reply. Still she passed anyway remembering the time she was left outside buzzing Nina's buzzer and ringing her phone on their lazy day date, not to mention when she passed by her work to discover Nina had been signed off sick and when she passed by her flat she wasn't there either.

Buzz! Buzz! No answer.

"She's not there." Jordan moaned slamming the passenger side door of the car as she got in.

"She's probably gone out then." Mark said abruptly not understanding what the big deal was. Little did he know it was a big deal to Jordan.

As they eventually arrived home and pulled up on their drive, Marks headlights caught the shadows of two people sitting on their house steps.

"Who is that?" They both asked in unison.

"You stay in the car baby I'll go and find out." Mark ordered Jordan, getting out the car and taking the steering wheel lock with him for a weapon just in case.

As he got out the car and started towards the steps he tried to work out who the two figures could possibly be and what they wanted. They both had hoods up as it was raining and one figure was taller than the other. In fact the smaller one looked like a kid.

Jordan was peering from the car trying to see what was happening and then she suddenly recognised one of the figures as he stood up and pulled his hood down revealing a mass of curly hair.

Alec.

"Mark wait!" Jordan shouted scrambling out of the car, "It's Alec one of my students."

Mark stopped in his tracks and turned to Jordan. "What? What is he doing here? What's going on Jordan?"

"I don't know Mark lets find out." Jordan was nervous now, the last thing she expected to come home to was this. She had already had a challenging day at Marks mothers.

Alec stepped forward with his arms around his kid brother.

"I'm so sorry to turn up at your home Miss. I didn't know where else to go. My mums gone missing and we've spent the entire day looking for her but had no luck. The house is empty and my little brother hasn't eaten and I have no money left and mum has taken the rest of the money for you know what. I wouldn't ask if I wasn't desperate but I have to go and find her. I know a few places she could be but they're too dangerous for Antoine to come with me. Could you watch him for me I'm begging you, please?"

"Whoa, slow down, shall we go inside and talk about this?" Mark said confused at all the goings on.

"I have to go! I'm sorry, I'll be back!" Alec shouted as he pulled his hood up over his hair and ran off disappearing into the darkness.

"I'll explain once we get inside." Jordan told Mark grabbing Antoine's small hand wondering where to start, dreading Marks reaction.

Jordan ran a bubble bath for Antoine, prepared him something to eat and made up the spare room for him. She read him a story and before long he was snoring softly. She stared at him and stroked his soft curly hair. It wasn't fair that this little boy had to go through this. He hadn't said a word apart from, "Please "and "Thank you." Jordan turned to leave the room bumping straight into Mark who was leaning in the doorway with his arms folded across his chest waiting for an explanation.

Jordan told Mark everything and every encounter she had had with Alec concerning the situation. She even told him about when she bumped into him at Club Sense when she was out with him and the 'Tree' meeting when Alec confessed about his mum's drug addiction.

Mark was astounded and angry that Jordan had become so deeply involved.

"This is a serious situation Jordan, really serious. It has to be declared and made formally known, it needs to go on record. You're putting your job on the line here." Mark told her straight.

Jordan didn't respond. She couldn't respond.

"You never thought about any of this did you?" He continued raising his voice. "You never even thought properly at all did you?" He was ashamed at her stupidity. "What hurts the most is that you kept me in the dark, you never thought to tell me. Is this the reason for your constant mood swings and distractions?"

Jordan could not gather up a group of words to even defend herself because she knew Mark was right. She felt silly and the truth was hurting her.

"It should not have got to these kids turning up on our doorstep! Let's just get the rest of today out of the way and hope Alec returns tonight.

Good job tomorrows Bank holiday hey?" With that said Mark got up and went to the bedroom leaving Jordan sitting by the lamp light on the sofa with the rain beating against the living room window. What had she done?

NINA.

Nina woke up with a pounding headache, still in last nights clothes with her shoes on the floor by her bed. She rubbed her eyes and tried to sit up and remember what had happened at the club. The memories were vague but one distinctive memory was that Jordan had branched out on her after behaving like a spoilt brat all night leaving her in the arms of . . . hazel eyes. Aaron. That was his name. They had caught a cab together. She looked at her shoes . . . he had rubbed her feet! She smiled and crawled to the bathroom for a cold shower in order to wake up.

Nina flung on some boy shorts, a wife beater and scraped up her wavy hair into a messy bun on top of her head before frying herself an omelette. It was Sunday so she decided to clean her flat whilst blasting Bob Marley. She plugged in both of her phones to charge and caught up on her emails before flopping back onto her bed for another rest. Nina closed her eyes and thought about work. Although tomorrow was a Bank holiday she had to work them as part of her contract. Roll on part time work she thought to herself excited at the prospect of actually having more time and freedom for herself.

Her work phone beeped and Nina looked at the clock on her bedside table, it read 3pm. It was a text from Frank, 'I hope you haven't forgotten our Sunday dinner date, meet me at TGI Fridays for 5pm, lets do casual for a change.'

Nina laughed, casual hey? She had forgotten that they had made plans but she didn't have any others and could do with more money towards her great plans.

Looking out of her bedroom window at the dull, grey sky Nina slipped on her black, DKNY, skinny jeans and a khaki coloured thermal top with her riding boots. She grabbed her Mack and stepped into her taxi. Her personal phone rang. Looking at the screen she didn't recognise the number but answered it anyway. "Hello?"

"Hi, is this Nina?" The voice on the other end of the phone asked.

"Speaking." She replied trying to figure out who she was talking to.

"It's Aaron." He said softly.

Nina smiled, "Hi Aaron, how are you doing?"

"Ah, so you remember me huh?" He said relieved that she wasn't to drunk the night before for him to become a puff of air. He really liked her and wanted to get to know her some more.

"Of course I remember you. Who could forget a foot massage as good as that? Or those beautiful eyes?" She complimented him.

"Well, erm . . . what are you up to today?" He asked blushing at her compliments and hoping to see her again sometime soon.

"I'm just on my way to meet a friend for dinner right about now," She admitted feeling bad, "Maybe in the week sometime?"

"How about tomorrow? It's Bank holiday?"

Nina laughed but Aaron didn't get it. "Unfortunately I have to work tomorrow its part of my contract." She told him.

"Ok so we aren't all privileged in that aspect then, no worries as you said maybe in the week."

"That would be nice." Nina agreed as they hung up.

Nina smiled for the rest of the cab ride to TGI's. She had butterflies in her stomach like she was a teenager again and it was all because of Aaron. From what she had encountered of him he was funny and charming, he seemed comfortable with himself in her presence and he was oh so handsome.

"Hey love, we're here." The driver woke her out of her daydream. Nina paid him and entered the restaurant.

Nina spotted Frank as soon as she walked in. It was a sight to see him in casual clothing, jeans and a shirt instead of a crisply, starched Versace suit and shiny shoes. He looked relaxed as he stood up and pulled a chair out for her to sit down.

They ordered gigantic burgers, fries, onion rings and salad as well as virgin cocktails. They finished off by sharing a desert. Nina was having a lovely time and she even noticed Frank smiling and laughing more than usual. Their other encounters seemed so business like and serious but today was different. It was warming.

"I have a surprise for you." Frank told Nina.

Curious yet nervous Nina asked what it was.

Frank requested the bill and told her she would have to wait and see as he escorted her to his Chrysler. The drive didn't seem long and from Nina's observations they were on the outskirts of Harborne. They pulled up to the gates of a very posh house. Frank pressed a few buttons and the gates opened allowing him onto the drive to park up. Frank got out and opened the passenger side helping Nina out admiring her dress sense.

"Wow Frank this house is beautiful." Nina said with her mouth wide open. She was unaware houses like this existed in Birmingham.

"This is just one of many of the properties I own," he boasted, "but enough, let us go inside and I'll show you your surprise."

Frank lead the way with Nina following behind admiring the art work and furnishings of what she had decided to call 'The Palace.' The house had a living room, dining room, a study, kitchen, conservatory, four bedrooms two of which were en suite and a separate bathroom and cloakroom. Nina wondered around in amazement at Franks elegant class and style.

"So is this the property you live in?" Nina asked nosily.

"No, not as a regular. It's to far out from my work and traffic is a nightmare in the mornings if I were to travel from here."

Nina nodded whilst listening, "That makes sense."

Frank grabbed Nina's hand and lead her upstairs to the Master bedroom for her to find a king-sized bed covered in rose petals with a large box wrapped in a red bow and a small box wrapped in a gold bow.

"Yes they are for you," Frank smiled, "but before you open them would you care to join me for a nice oil bath?"

It's not like Nina had any reason to refuse and she had to remember he was paying her for her time and to satisfy his desires.

So they shared a candle lit, aromatherapy oil bath and Frank surprised her further with a Victoria Secrets all in one body suit. They both sat on the king-sized bed and Nina discovered the contents of the boxes. The large box contained a pair of Prada stilettos' and the small box had a white gold Swarovski crystal necklace inside. Nina didn't know what to say as she felt Frank secure the necklace around her neck. She knew what he was up to. He was trying to buy her affections with material things. He thought he could mess with her feelings.

"Why Frank?" Nina asked.

"Why what?" He replied, pretending he didn't know what she was getting at.

"Why the gifts Frank?" She spelled it out for him clearly,

"Because you provide me with a high quality service. You always look wonderful and smell good, keep appointments and time and most importantly perform well, very well. Let's just call it gratitude and appreciation, a tip maybe."

Nina didn't know how to feel and wanted to put him straight. "I am very grateful for your kind gestures Frank but working and getting paid for it is enough for me."

"I did not intend to offend you in any way," Frank apologised, "let's not spoil the arrangement we have it works well."

He crawled over to her and stroked her legs planting kisses up her inner thighs knowing that was what she liked.

Nina arrived home at 11pm that night with her gifts in hand. She had really enjoyed her evening but was becoming more nervous regarding the Frank situation. She had to call Claire definitely and stop putting it off before it got out of hand. She felt a hint of guilt as Aaron crossed her mind. But it still didn't stop her slipping her Prada heels on and strutting up and down her hallway the fashionista she was, grinning like a Cheshire cat.

Nina packed her work bag and made her sandwiches for her return to work. She set out a black fitted pinafore dress she had purchased. Dressing to impress to entice Mr Allen to give her part time hours, she was bad. Who knew, she might even wear her new Prada heels.

As she got into bed Nina realised she could never become close to Aaron, not when she was an Escort. "I cannot get attached." She told herself.

9

JORDAN.

I T WAS 2AM and Mark sat at the kitchen table with his head in his hands.

"Where's Alec?"

Mark looked up to see Antoine standing in the kitchen doorway staring at Mark with his innocent gray eyes clutching a teddy bear.

"Hey little man, you should be sleeping." Mark told him.

"I want Alec," Antoine moaned, "I can't sleep without him."

Mark felt bad for the young boy, having been dragged from pillar to post not quite understanding what was actually occurring.

"I'll tell you what, I'll make us both a great big hot chocolate with marshmallows on the top to help us go to sleep and when you wake up Alec should be here. How about that?" Mark proposed hoping it would work.

Antoine nodded his head holding on tight to the teddy that Jordan had found for him as Mark lifted him up and placed him on to a chair at the kitchen table. As they both sat at the table sipping their hot chocolate's Mark was tempted to ask Antoine so many questions but knew that would be unfair on him. He was just a kid.

Antoine's eyes started drooping and his head flopping. Mark chuckled, "Come on little man." He scooped him up and wiped the froth from his top lip with the tea towel and started up the stairs.

"I don't want to go to bed." Antoine stirred.

"Ok then." Mark said carrying him into the living room. He was tired himself. As he lay back on the sofa Antoine snuggled up next to him and before long they were both out like a light.

It was 8am as Jordan made her way downstairs after checking all the rooms upstairs and finding no one present.

Bingo! Sound asleep on the living room sofa was her husband with Antoine resting on his stomach sucking his thumb. Jordan stood admiring the two before heading into the kitchen to make some breakfast. She was disappointed that Alec hadn't returned and had left Antoine in their care. He would be awake soon, what was she supposed to tell him?

Throughout the rest of the morning Jordan enjoyed watching how Mark interacted with Antoine feeling assured that he would make a good father.

"You're good with him." Jordan complimented hoping to put a smile on his face.

Mark wasn't interested in her small talk. "Listen Jordan," Mark said quietly through gritted teeth, "It's called occupying him, distracting him until his brother comes back, if he comes back! How do we know he hasn't taken us for a couple of fools?"

Jordan stormed off into the kitchen feeling ashamed but Mark had not finished yet. He left Antoine watching Shrek 2 and followed Jordan, hot on her heels. "The moment Alec arrives here this will be passed on to the system. His mother needs re-hab and Antoine needs stable, safe and secure accommodation. Alec is old enough to make decisions concerning himself."

Mark decided to take Antoine to the Sea Life Centre and then for dinner at Nando's that afternoon, leaving Jordan at home to wait for Alec. Although the case Mark and Antoine returned home still to no sign of Alec. They didn't have any contact number for him either.

"This is ridiculous!" Mark said packing a case up. He was going away to Scotland for a school trip tomorrow for a few days. "I can't go away and leave this situation how it is." He was really frustrated that he had had to spend his Bank holiday weekend entertaining Jordan's mess.

Just then there was a loud banging at the front door. Mark ran to open it to find Alec with scratches all over his face and dirt all over his hoody.

"What happened?" Mark asked pushing him into the kitchen so Antoine didn't get a chance to see him in such a state.

"Where's Antoine." was Alec's main concern.

"He's asleep," Jordan cut in, "He's fine."

Alec told Mark and Jordan how he had searched all night for his mother and was going to give up and make his way back when he spotted her on a street corner trying to sell herself in order to make enough money for a quick fix. Tears poured out of his eyes as he continued to tell them how he had tried to drag her away to get her some help but she attacked him and tried to escape. Alec had reached the point of breaking down and Mark felt a lump in his throat but he had to hold it together.

Alec explained how he had taken her to the nearest hospital kicking and screaming and told them about her addiction. "I know you both have lives of your own and I cannot expect you to look after Antoine so I did what I should have done ages ago. Social services are coming at 9pm to collect us both. I gave them your address. I'm so sorry for putting you both through this."

Jordan went upstairs to the bathroom and cried her heart out.

"Listen," Mark told Alec, "you did what you thought was right and that's all that matters. That was one of the toughest things you have ever had to do and you did it. The rest will follow now. You're a brave man." Mark praised him and patted his back. "Go and have a shower, I'll get you one of my clean jogging suits and other stuff and make you something to eat before Social services get here."

Mark felt a sense of relief followed by pity, but it was for the best. What did Jordan think was going to happen? Antoine helped Mark prepare some food, excited that his big brother was back.

Alec made his way into the spare room to dry off and get changed after his shower when he bumped into Jordan. She was tidying away the duvet. "Oh sorry Alec." She said turning around.

Alec grabbed her by the hand with only his towel around his waist and water droplets dripping on to his chest from his curly, wet hair. "I just wanted to say thank you." His gray eyes pierced through her causing her to feel uneasy. She shifted her hand free from his grasp politely and looked around the room trying to avoid eye contact.

"I'm sorry Alec, about your mother and everything you have had to go through. I think it was inevitable it would up end this way, but it's for the best and I am proud of you. I'll write my numbers down for Social services to keep in contact with me. Keep me updated. If you or Antoine need anything make sure you ask." Jordan bent down to pick up Antoine's teddy and as she stood up Alec grabbed her face and kissed her lips gently.

Jordan was shocked. "Alec! What are you playing at?" She whispered harshly, "My husband is downstairs Alec. HUSBAND!" And with that she marched out of the room.

Social Services arrived at 9pm on the dot and they all said their goodbyes. Jordan was touched at the relationship Mark had built up with Antoine in such a short period of time. Antoine clung to Marks neck and Mark gave him a goody bag of his favourite snacks to take with him and his adopted tatty teddy. Alec thanked them both looking at Jordan all the while.

"Take good care." Mark waved them off.

Mark held Jordan tight that night as they lay in bed together knowing he was going away the next day for a while. He was one of those people who liked to leave on a positive and happy note.

"Listen babes, it's been a crazy weekend but it's over now, back to normality. I know you are upset but it'll soon pass, it was for the best." He said kissing her forehead before closing his eyes yearning for sleep.

Jordan just held on to him a little bit tighter for a little bit longer and closed her eyes.

NINA.

Nina was ready and dressed for work at 8:30 am keen to stay on Mr Allen's good side so he would give her the hours she wanted. She drove up the Hagley road singing along to White Stripes with a big smile on her face regardless of it being Bank Holiday Monday.

"Good morning Mr Allen." She chirped as she headed towards her office. It was exactly how she had left it apart from a few extra files that had been placed on her desk.

"Good morning Nina," Mr Allen replied looking her up and down then down and up, noticing how her pinafore dress hugged curves he never knew she had. In fact he had to turn away to control his funny feelings. "It's nice to have you back."

Nina smiled and began organising her work load to catch up.

"Shall we do your return to work at 11am? Give you a chance to settle down." He asked Nina.

Nina wasn't familiar with return to work papers and interviews as she never had time off sick. The more she thought about things she realised how prim and proper she actually had been. She must have been a boring sod. Never sick, always on time, always working, turning her nose up at this and that, the list was endless and in just two weeks so much of that had changed.

Mr Allen showed great concern to the fact that Nina had been signed off with stress considering she always had a calm and methodical approach to her work. He had no choice but to put it down to personal problems or her home life. He valued her as his employee and was quite shocked when she cut to the chase and requested part time hours.

"How many days a week would suit you?" He asked her a little upset to be partially loosing his hardest worker.

"Three." Nina replied with certainty.

"How about three and a half?" Mr Allen tried to barter.

Nina laughed, "Would that half make a difference?" She enquired.

"To myself and the business needs . . . yes definitely." He told her trying to send her on a guilt trip as if she would be leaving him in the lurch.

"Ok. Now to decide which three and a half days." Nina queried.

Nina felt a slightly bad for putting Mr Allen on the spot but she had to do what was best for her. In the past two weeks she had never been happier. She was just trying to find a balance in her life. A happy balance.

An agreement was finally made for Nina to work Mondays, Wednesdays, Thursdays and until midday on Fridays. She was satisfied as she could enjoy extended weekends to have fun and work her secret life.

"I'll sort the paper work out and we'll get you in your part time position as of . . ."

"Next week!" Nina butted in finishing off Mr Allen's sentence.

Mr Allen glared at Nina in an inquisitive manner. "Why do you want to work part time at your age and all of a sudden?"

"Lets just say I had two weeks to think about things and reflect on my life and where I want it to go, what I want to achieve and experience. I'm going to be thirty years of age soon and I need change. Do you understand that?" She asked him, expecting an answer.

"Totally, I went through a stage like that in my life at around your age." He confided in her. "You need to do what's best for you, we only have one life so make the most of it."

Driving home that evening from work Nina felt contented. She hadn't expected Mr Allen to be so supportive and understanding towards her request for part time hours. She also felt a sense of value and appreciation from him to. Maybe while she was off for two weeks reflecting on life he may have carried out a little bit of life reflecting himself.

Pulling up into the car park of her apartment complex, Nina noticed a silver Audi A3 parked up. She had never seen that car there before. She stepped out of her Mini and hauled her work bag out of the boot.

"Hey sexy lady." A voice whispered in her ear. She felt the lips brush against her earlobe and she spun around in fright.

"Aaron! You scared me!" She screamed pushing him playfully. "What you doing here?"

Aaron held a big, brown paper bag in his arms and a bottle of wine. Nina didn't know whether to be pleased or not. Really she was yearning for a quiet night in with a hot bubble bath and junk food. She hated when people just turned up.

"If Mohammed cannot get to the mountain, the mountain will come to Mohammed." He grinned. "Everyone deserves a Bank holiday so I bought us some Chinese food, I hope you don't mind?"

He was really chuffed with his little surprise and Nina didn't want to burst his bubble so she invited him into her flat. She kicked off her Prada heels and Aaron followed suite removing his Adidas trainers.

"The kitchen is straight ahead Aaron, there should be some plates and glasses on the dish rack." Nina directed and pointed. "I'm just going to dump these in the office and freshen up, make yourself comfy."

Aaron found what was necessary and Nina helped him carry the goodies into the living room. She went to put the TV on and Aaron stopped her. "I never came to watch TV." He said looking at her as if he was going to eat her up instead of his food. "I came to get to know you a little bit better,"

Nina was starving and it was quite obvious causing Aaron to laugh at her and dish more food out on to her plate. "I like a girl that can eat." He smirked.

"You wouldn't be saying that if I blew up."

"But you keep it tight." Aaron beamed.

Nina blushed.

Aaron continued firing the comments and compliments at Nina causing her cheeks to go red. "You look so nice and classy in your work wear. I like how you carry yourself, and how you keep your home."

Nina learnt that Aaron worked a nine to five at Audi sometimes doing overtime on weekends. He was thirty one and didn't have any children which she couldn't quite believe. He had been single for nearly two years after a five year relationship with a girl who used him as an ATM (that's how he put it) and stayed unemployed with no aim and ambition. Refusing to stay with someone like that he decided to move on.

"I want a lady that is hardworking, independent, bright and beautiful. I think I'm sitting next her right this moment." He told Nina, leaning forward, brushing her hair out of her face and placing his soft lips against hers. Nina felt shivers flood down her spine.

"No pressure then?" She joked, wondering if he really meant what he said.

Nina mentioned the basic things about herself and her life. She didn't mention her reduction in hours at work. She didn't intend to become attached to Aaron but he was messing with her feelings immensely and he knew it. She did really like him but deep down she knew she could not let him into her life especially being an Escort and a newly qualified one at that. Life had just begun for Nina and she had to stay focused.

"So are you going to tell me your age?" Aaron asked Nina. "Don't ask me to guess because I'm no good like that." He informed her.

"I'll be thirty in two weeks." Nina whispered at him as if people were around to hear such a secret.

Aaron twisted up his face. "Your lying. You look about twenty five."

"Why thank you," Nina laughed, "flattery will take you to far places."

Aaron admired how silly Nina could be. He loved seeing her smile and laugh. "I hope so."

"I'm just going to take the plates into the kitchen." Nina said standing up and fixing her pinafore.

As Nina got up to do so Aaron noticed her perfectly manicured nails and toes, her dark features against her caramel complexion, perfectly groomed eyebrows, the beauty spot on the top of her lip on the right side and her thick wavy hair with the baby hairs resting against her forehead. He was really feeling her.

The evening had come to an end and surprisingly Nina had had a pleasant time. "Thank you for such a lovely evening it was a nice surprise."

"You're welcome." Aaron told her crouching down to lace up his trainers. "Prada?" He said noticing the label on Nina's shoes sitting on the mat at her front door.

"I have a little bit of a shoe fetish." she confirmed hoping he wouldn't pry any further about the expense.

They kissed goodnight and Aaron got into his car and drove off. He wanted so badly to make her his but he knew if he pushed to hard to soon, he would end up pushing her away. "Slow your role." He told himself as he carried on home.

Nina enjoyed a long shower with her cranberry body wash followed by baby oil. She climbed into bed feeling joyous and giddy inside. She knew Aaron really liked her and the feeling was undeniably mutual. Nina started questioning herself. "Why did this have to happen now? I just decide to make adjustments to my life and 'Mr Perfect' appears." As she lay her head down on her pillow she made a decision to step back from Aaron and create a distance between them so he eventually would become bored of the chase and let go.

Little did she know it wasn't going to be that easy.

10

JORDAN.

I<small>T WAS WEDNESDAY</small> morning as Jordan made her way downstairs to collect the post off the mat. Some of her students were on study leave so she didn't have to be at work until later that afternoon. She always anticipated this time of year as it gave her opportunity to catch up on her workload but every time it did actually arrive she wished it was the beginning of the school year again.

She picked the post up off the mat and noticed a letter for Mark with a stamp on it indicating it was from the hospital. "Hospital?" She questioned respecting his privacy and dropping it on his desk with the pile of other letters that had arrived throughout the week for him. Her train of thought was broken by the ringing of the house phone. She answered to find it was Social Services updating her on Alec and Antoine's progress in the system as well as their mother's progress with her rehabilitation therapy. Jordan was made up that the news was positive and they were being catered and cared for, especially Antoine. She thought he'd be unsettled without Alec around constantly. Alec had been given options and had opted to be placed in a hostel until they could find him a place of his own and he went to see Antoine everyday without fail.

Jordan jumped into the shower. She wanted to get some grocery shopping done before she went to work. As she got ready she thought about Mark being away on his school trip and really how grateful she was for his absence. After all that had happened recently she felt the time apart would be healthy for their relationship.

Stepping into her Kurt Geiger's and grabbing her bag and keys Jordan headed out of her front door coming face to face with Alec.

"Alec!" She gasped shocked. "What are you doing here?"

Alec gave her that dreaded look. That deep, penetrating stare as if she was transparent and he could see everything, even down to her emotions.

"I just popped around knowing you wouldn't be in class this morning due to study leave and to say thank you for what you did for me and Antoine on the weekend. You and your husband didn't have to and we really appreciated it, Antoine won't stop talking about Mark." He said handing Jordan a bunch of flowers.

"Thank you very much, you didn't have to. Social services have just called me this morning updating me on your family's progress, I'm glad things are gradually falling into place I'll be sure to tell my husband." She said nervously, shutting the front door and locking it.

"Aren't you going to put the flowers in water?" Alec questioned. "Or are you in a hurry?"

Jordan felt ambushed and caught off guard. Alec made her feel uneasy and uncomfortable especially since the episode in the spare bedroom on Monday night.

"Ten minutes Alec. You can tell me what you've been up to and you're future plans whilst I arrange the flowers."

She lead Alec through to the kitchen dropping her bag and keys on the kitchen table and getting a vase out of the cupboard. Alec leaned against the counter top next to her watching her trimming the stems of the flowers.

"So tell me where you are staying and what it's like." Jordan broke the awkward silence.

Alec told Jordan about the hostel he was staying in and how supportive they were to him. He also mentioned the fact that he wanted his own place in case his mother relapsed again. That way Antoine could stop with him.

Jordan wasn't quite sure how the system worked regarding situations like that so she never passed a comment. He had it all planned out in his head and she wasn't about to introduce any negative energy.

"What about your studies?" She asked handing him the vase so he could fill it with some water.

"Well that's where you come into the equation." He grinned handing her back the vase filled with some water.

Jordan knew what he was playing at and thought quickly.

"How about we make an appointment for you to have a meeting with myself and the head teacher back at school to discuss your options and get you through then?"

Alec didn't answer. He handed her the last flower, the rose.

Jordan took it and placed it in the vase.

"The middle would be the best place for the rose." He said stretching his arm around Jordan to reposition it.

Jordan turned around with the vase in her hands ready to make her way to the dining room to place it at the centre of the table.

Alec took the vase from her hands and placed it back on the kitchen counter top staring deeply into her eyes, up close in her personal capacity.

"Alec, I want them in the dining room." She laughed wondering what he was playing at and feeling even more uneasy trying to edge away.

"And I want you." He said suddenly kissing her passionately on her lips.

Jordan responded by returning the kiss long and hard. She was fully aware of what she was doing. She had longed for Alec's wanting kiss since he tried to kiss her on the Monday but with Mark in the house the deceit was a clear reality slapping her in the face.

Alec started removing Jordan's clothes as she removed his. He carried her into the living room planting kisses all over her body all the while gazing into her eyes. He wanted to touch and feel every part of her and she could feel the affections oozing from him as he did so. He lay her down gently on the sofa, tracing the contours of her body with his fingers, biting and sucking on her sensitive areas, areas Mark overlooked or never took the time to become familiar with. Nothing was said as Alec retrieved a condom from his jeans pocket and placed it on. He entered Jordan kissing her on her eyes, then nose and last but not least on her lips as he thrust in and out of her with gentle strokes. Jordan closed her eyes with guilt but pleasure, she couldn't fight the feeling. She knew what was occurring right there on her sofa was wrong but there seemed no point in stopping it now as the damage was already done. Alec gripped her body tightly and they shuddered at the same time. She felt him breath deeply into her neck. They gazed into each others eyes as if trying to figure out each others thoughts.

Jordan went to the bathroom upstairs and Alec used the downstairs one to clean up when he noticed the condom had broken.

"Jordan!" He shouted up the stairs.

"Not now Alec!" She shouted back.

As they left the house Alec tried again to let Jordan know about the burst condom. "Jordan the . . ."

"Alec, please don't. Let's pretend this never happened, it shouldn't have happened, I should not have let it happen." She scolded herself.

"I'm sorry Jordan." Alec said and walked away.

Jordan got into her car. What had she done?

Mark would be home on Friday, then what?

NINA.

Nina could not wait for the following week when her part time hours would begin. Unfortunately she had to get through this week working full time hours for Mr Allen and managing her clients around it. She didn't want to loose their business and it was just for one week she reminded herself.

On top of that Aaron was becoming an issue. He wanted to be her boyfriend, her man, he wanted her for himself. Amidst her busy schedule for that week she clearly could not delegate time to him and she knew that by the weekend she would have to face him and inform him that this was how it would be to try to put him off. Would she tell him not to bother pursuing her or give in and carry on regardless keeping her secret life the secret it was?

"Wake up beautiful." Frank whispered into Nina's ear planting kisses on her cheek.

Nina opened her eyes realising she wasn't in her own bed, remembering she had spent the night at Franks apartment in the city centre.

"I should have been up preparing that for you." She told Frank as he handed her a breakfast tray containing croissants, eggs and juice.

Frank had desperately wanted an appointment with Nina and was grateful that she had slotted him in last minute. They compromised that she stay over at his and make her way to work the following morning from there to ease the pressure of her hectic diary. He had agreed to pay extra for her time grateful that he would be waking up to her for once as if she belonged to him.

Nina took it for what it was, work. She stayed and satisfied his desires that night and once more that morning before heading to work.

"Can I drop you to work?" Frank offered.

"Thanks Frank but you know my rules."

"I respect that." He smiled, "At least let me call you a cab then?"

"That would be great." With that sorted out Nina picked up her envelope and headed out the door.

Frank admired her as she left wishing she was solely his.

Nina strolled into work smiling after having good quality sleep in Franks king sized bed. "Morning." She sang as she headed towards her office.

"Somebody's happy." Mr Allen said watching her skip along.

Really she wanted to scream out from the top of her lungs; "Yesterday I stayed in a plush apartment, ate the finest cuisine, drank expensive wine and had great sex last night before bed and this morning before work and I got a paid!" But she knew she could never do that and giggled to herself at the thought of it.

Later that afternoon Mr Allen announced that their weekly meeting would be held at a restaurant he knew very well. It was to be his treat that Friday after work and they were to make a night of it. Nina and the other staff could not believe it, never had Mr Allen taken them out in the six years she had worked for him, all expenses paid. She also knew the reduction of her hours would be a topic of discussion in the meeting. She had to prepare herself for the inquisitive minds of her colleagues.

"Where's your car?" Clare, one of Nina's colleagues asked her as they clocked out of work that evening.

"In the garage." Nina replied, prepared with her answer from that morning for the nosey soul that would ask.

"Do you want a lift?" She asked.

"No thanks Clare, I'm going to my friends for dinner and it would be out of your way, but thanks for the offer."

Really if Clare had dropped Nina home she would've clearly seen her Mini parked on the drive in front of her flat and it would be apparent Nina was lying.

Nina decided to call Jordan and see if she was up for an evening together. They hadn't spent time since club Boujee and as Mark was away it was her duty to look out for her best friend.

She caught a cab home from work that evening and unpacked her overnight bag whilst on the phone to Jordan.

"Hey Jordan, how about some company this evening?"

"That would be nice." Jordan said grateful that Nina would be rescuing her from spending time with her own conscious. "What do you have in mind?"

"Take out and chat? Or home cooking and reminiscing?"

"The second option please." Jordan said excitedly.

Nina dragged on her Adidas jogging suit and trainers and got into her car when her personal phone rang. The caller ID read Aaron. She stared at the screen contemplating whether to answer it or not. She left it to reach voice mail and headed to Jordan's.

Nina and Jordan cooked curry fish and prawns with basmati rice and naan bread.

"Isn't it funny how life goes?" Jordan said scooping up some of her curry using a piece of her naan bread wanting so badly to tell Nina about the trials and tribulations herself and Mark had encountered Bank holiday weekend and her guilty secret concerning Alec. She decided against the idea, the thought of Alec made her stomach ache and eating curry wasn't a helpful aid at all.

"Isn't it just." Nina agreed with a mouthful of food thinking about her secret life and if Jordan or her family found out how they would react? Would they throw up a dictionary of demeaning words to label her out of disgust? Or would they surprisingly see the attraction and want in? Never she thought to herself, dream on.

Jordan enquired about Aaron instead to lighten the mood.

"So, how's hazel eyes?"

Nina laughed, "You mean Aaron?" She corrected her.

"I want to know what's going on between the two of you?" Jordan asked getting straight to the point.

"Meaning, have we met up since club Boujee? Have we slept together? If so was it good? Are you an item?" Nina said giggling and teasing Jordan by depriving her of the information that would be the be all and end all.

"Yes, yes, yes and yes!" Jordan laughed back.

Nina told Jordan how the night out at club Boujee ended and how Aaron surprised her the Bank holiday Monday.

"He clearly likes you, sounds as if he has got it bad to. Do you have the 'Love Jones'?" Jordan asked Nina taking a sip of water to cool her mouth down from the curry.

"It's way to early to label it as love but I do like him, he's a really nice hardworking, attentive guy, but I'm not quite sure what I want right about now concerning relationships and commitment. I don't want to string him along."

"So you're going to ignore him like you usually do to the guys who show an interest in you, in hope of him becoming fed up of the chase and then he'll let go?" Jordan knew how Nina played it, she knew her like the back of her hand.

"Don't say that!" Nina said feeling ashamed that Jordan had her sussed.

"Well I'm only being truthful. You do it all the time Nina and you know I'm right so do not look at me like that." Jordan laughed.

"I just have a lot going on right about now." Nina told Jordan half the truth.

"Like?" Jordan looked at her wondering what could possibly be taking up her valuable time.

"A career change, maybe study again. Oh I'm not sure. Just sorting out my life I guess." Nina shoved more food into her mouth to shut herself up in hope of delaying the conversation or indicating the need to close it, full stop.

"He could be that part of your life that makes your future something great, fills that void. You've been single for a while now." Jordan told her as if she didn't know.

Nina changed the subject abruptly. "What have you got planned for my birthday?" She asked Jordan giddy with excitement. It was tradition that they made the birthday plans for each others birthdays.

"You'll know by Sunday evening the latest." Jordan confirmed trying to hide her panic. With all the goings on she had forgotten how soon Nina's birthday actually was and it was her big three zero.

"Wash or dry?" Jordan asked Nina.

"Dry." Nina said catching the tea towel as Jordan threw it at her.

The girls called it a night and Nina's work phone rang as she made her way down Jordan's steps to her car.

"That's not your ring tone." Jordan said ear wigging.

"New phone!" Nina shouted getting into her Mini. "Nosey cow!" She mumbled underneath her breath before answering.

Ryan, one of her clients wanted a late night appointment tomorrow when he finished his limo shift.

As Nina lay her head amongst her mountain of pillows that night her personal phone beeped. It was a text from Aaron. 'Hey miss busy body, just wanted to check you are ok, hope to catch up with you this weekend, goodnite x.'

She sighed confused about what to do. She really liked him and if her secret life was non existent and she held down her standard nine to five at Mr Allen's like she had three weeks ago she would allow him into her life effortlessly. Pursuing a relationship with Aaron and holding down her secret life would feel like cheating and if it came out, which she knew it would eventually (as one cannot hide things like that from their partner) the affects would be devastating.

"Why did you make an appearance now Aaron? Why not four weeks ago?" She said staring at the ceiling trying to figure her thoughts out.

11

JORDAN.

Grateful that it was Friday, Jordan tied up her loose ends at work and hurried to her car excited for Marks return.

As she made her way to her car she noticed Alec leaning against her drivers side door.

"What are you doing?" Jordan asked making it clear that his presence was not appreciated.

"Jordan, I really have to talk to you." He said.

Jordan's heart started to beat heavily like a bass drum and she heard the echoing through her ears. Alec standing in front of her made her realise how much of a mistake she had made yesterday. She had slept with one of her students! A fresh tonne of guilt dropped down on her conscious making her feel like running. But where would she run to? And it would be the same when she returned.

"Alec, not today, in fact never. I just want to go home and spend some time with my husband." Jordan stated loud and clear.

"Jordan but it's important . . ."

"Stop it Alec!" She shouted becoming irritated by his persistence. "What happened was a mistake, get over it!" She said loading her bags into the boot of the car and slamming it shut.

"Ok." Alec said walking off not prepared to cause a scene. "Lets hope it doesn't end up an even bigger one." He mumbled under his breath watching Jordan get into her car and drive off.

"This is all my fault." She told herself whilst driving suddenly not wanting to go home anymore.

Jordan entered the house to find Mark in the office sifting through his mail from the past week.

"Hey baby." She said wrapping her arms around his shoulders and kissing the back of his head playing pretend.

Mark spun around slowly on his office chair and positioned her on his lap kissing her long and hard.

"How's my lady been? Did you miss me?" He asked admiring her face and looking into her eyes.

"Loads." Jordan smiled hugging him tightly to try and indicate how much.

"What's the plan to celebrate my return?" Mark teased.

"Anything you want to do."

"Well in that case, take away and sexy time, we have a lot of making up to do!" He laughed rubbing her thighs.

"Chinese or Indian?" Jordan asked with an aching heart.

NINA.

"Let's go then people!" Mr Allen shouted outside their place of work as a few taxi's pulled up to carry them off to the fancy restaurant he had picked for their weekly meeting and combined night out.

All of the staff were prepared to make the most of this night, after all it was once in a blue moon Mr Allen treated them to an all expenses paid outing. Driving was not on the agenda, strictly drinking hence the line of taxi's.

The taxi's pulled up outside a very familiar restaurant in the Jewellery Quarter. Nina's heart skipped a beat as she realised Mr Allen's favourite restaurant was Frank's Place. She took a deep breath and reassured herself that she would be alright.

"Are you alright Nina?" Nosey Clare asked her.

"I'm fine, just hungry that's all." She told her.

Nina noticed Frank at the entrance greeting her workforce and pointing them in the direction of their table for the night all the while laughing with Mr Allen as if they were the best of friends.

She wanted so badly to run and hide but she knew her absence would draw unwanted attention. No one was aware of the situation she had with Frank and they didn't have to be. She hoped Frank would maintain his professional and respectful demeanour by not letting on otherwise.

Nina approached him last noticing the glint in his eyes. He shook her hand just like he had the rest of the staff and pointed her in the direction of a large table laid out especially for them that evening.

Before letting her go he gripped her hand tightly and whispered gently in her ear, "Fancy this. You look lovely as usual. I'll catch up with you sometime during the night I hope . . . Sunshine."

"Thank you." Nina said before heading toward the table maintaining her composure as best as she could.

The evening progressed nicely and as Nina suspected her reduction in working hours was a topic of discussion as were a few promotions and Mr Allen informing them of how well the business was doing, hence the party and him feeling the need to splash the cash on them all.

They had dined on the finest cuisine and with full stomachs made their way to the bar area and lounge to drink plenty and be merry. Nina was really enjoying herself, the atmosphere was buzzing as she swayed to the Jazz music the live band were playing so well. She was in her element.

Mr Allen made his way up to Nina placing a Cosmopolitan in her empty hand.

"I don't want to see any empty hands or glasses." He said in a drunken state. "So, are you enjoying yourself? Cuz I am." He laughed grooving to the music out of rhythm.

"Definitely." Nina replied trying not to laugh at him. "It's been a really nice evening, thank you very much Mr Allen."

"Yes, but it's thanks to my cousin Frank really." He told her, propping himself up on the bar.

Nina choked on her drink as it flowed down the wrong hole.

"Are you ok?" Mr Allen asked patting her back as if he intended to break it.

"Yes . . . yes thanks." She spluttered trying to compose herself all embarrassed.

"I think my cousin likes you." Mr Allen continued.

"What makes you think that?" Nina asked becoming nervous and paranoid at what Mr Allen knew concerning her and Frank. She continued to play non the wiser.

"He keeps admiring you. He's a good guy my cousin . . . he's not attached either you know . . . in fact you and him would fit together nicely."

Little did Mr Allen know Nina and Frank had tessellated very nicely on many occasions.

It started getting late as one by one the staff descended home. Nina made her way to the ladies before planning on doing the same. As she did so Frank met her in the corridor grabbed her gently by her hand and took her up the stairs to his office. Locking the door and closing the blinds, he drew her body close to his and held her around the waist.

"I'm not on duty Frank." She informed him gently pushing him away.

"Could you be?" He asked yearning for her, pulling her back to him.

"Not tonight, but we could make other arrangements for another time." She said trying to stay professional yet firm. "I am at a works do which you know as Mr Allen is your cousin." She couldn't help but let on that she knew that fact.

"That's right . . . Nina." He breathed hard at her staring straight into her eyes.

Nina felt pressured and her privacy invaded by the one person she wanted to keep at arms length safely and securely. Not only was Frank related closely to her employer, he knew her place of work and now her real name thanks to Mr Allen. What next?

"I have to go to the bathroom, excuse, me." Nina said releasing his grip feeling a little nauseas.

"Don't worry I won't say anything. I want our arrangement to remain the same. You are my Sunshine and you satisfy me in ways I love and am quite happy to continue paying for." Frank reassured her.

"Thank you Frank." Nina smiled a smile of relief and gratitude, thankful for his sensible attitude. With that said she hurried off back to the party.

"Sunshine, before you go, I just want to let you know you impress me more each time with your beauty, class and elegance and to discover how hard you work shows the aim, ambition and standards you set yourself. You are quite a woman. Why do you escort?"

Nina felt the need to answer in order to stop the subtle harassment once and for all with sheer clarity.

"Because I have just me, myself and I. I have no commitments or responsibilities and the excitement and adventure makes me feel alive. The money is good allowing me to save as well as be frivolous and have the finer things in life and the busy lifestyle doesn't leave room for loneliness to become a friend. Is that a good enough set of reasons for you?" She asked holding his gaze.

"But I could provide all of that for you and more with sincerity." He claimed.

"That's nice Frank but it's not what I want or am prepared for right about now. I'm content as I am thank you."

"Sure."

With that said Nina left Franks office in hope of never having to mention it again.

12

JORDAN.

JORDAN ROLLED OVER to Mark's empty side of the bed. He had popped into work that Saturday morning to prepare for the week ahead as he had been away to Scotland on a school trip. She had noticed that he had tidied his desk. Impressed with his organisation she sat at his desk instead of hers and surfed the internet for some last minute city breaks for Nina's birthday. With nothing else planned she got lost in Barcelona, Venice and Paris.

She thought about cooking a birthday meal for Nina with herself, Mark and even 'Hazel eyes' present. Laughing at the thought of it as well as feeling chuffed with the idea she went into the kitchen to make herself some breakfast.

"Ahhhh!" She gasped as she saw Alec's piercing gray eyes glaring at her through the kitchen window, but after blinking once or twice she realised it was all in her mind.

"Get a grip!" She told herself.

Feeling spooked out and no longer wanting to spend the day alone she rang Nina to see what she was up to.

"Hello." Nina answered groggily.

"Late night?" Jordan guessed.

"Yes, works do, courtesy of Mr Allen. Yes I know shock, shock horror." Nina laughed into her pillow. "So, what's the matter?"

"I just didn't fancy being alone today, Mark's gone to work for a bit to catch up on some work so I thought I could spend some time with you and run through your birthday plans?"

Unlike Jordan, Nina was looking forward to spending the day by herself but sensed how tender Jordan was. "Ok, give me an hour or so to sort myself out and come over."

NINA.

Nina was knackered. Finally the weekend had showed it's face ending her congested week. Thankful and looking forward to the beginning of a new life, with partial routine she rolled over hunting through her pillows to answer her personal phone that was ringing. It was Jordan wanting to spend the day discussing birthday plans.

Frank and Aaron both wanted to spend time with her that evening but having had enough of Frank from the night before she opted for a date with Aaron. After all she had a lot to sort out with him regarding the next level of their 'relationship' if that's what it was.

Frank could wait until Sunday.

Dragging herself out of bed and having a good old stretch, she got a move on tidying up her place. Jordan was the punctual type and an hour or so was one hour exactly in Jordan's book.

Jordan arrived dead on time just as Nina had predicted with a bottle of Mexican lime crush in hand, Nina's favourite.

Nina shared the dramatics and the jokes of the works party with Jordan, entertaining her by doing impressions of a drunken Mr Allen. They spent ages rolling around on the floor laughing like a couple of kids. After wearing themselves out and getting hyperactive from the Mexican lime crush, they tackled the serious issue of Nina's birthday plans.

"So make sure those dates are logged into your diary!" Jordan shouted to Nina from the living room.

"Oh it's in my bedroom on my bedside table." Nina shouted back from the bathroom.

"I'll go and get it." Jordan said scrambling into Nina's bedroom. Jordan just wanted to be nosey at what new shoes and clothes she could find of Nina's to beg, borrow or steal. She had noticed how she had been living a bit of a 'Diva' lifestyle lately and wanted in. She flicked through Nina's diary trying to find the week she needed and noticed in previous weeks Nina had kept appointments with a 'Frank', 'Ryan', and 'Clive'. But Frank seemed to be the most popular. She also noticed, in big writing scrawled across the coming week, 'part time hours' with a big smiling face.

"Have you found it?" Nina shouted catching Jordan off guard entering her bedroom.

Jordan quickly closed the diary in shock and stood up. "Yep I got it, I was admiring your Prada shoes. They must have cost a bomb?"

Nina didn't grant Jordan a response, she took her diary from Jordan's hands and went into the living room to enter the necessary dates. As she did so her personal phone beeped. It was a text from Aaron.

"Ooh, is that 'hazel eyes'? Jordan hissed grinning. "Don't forget to give him the date and time for your birthday meal." She reminded her.

"How could I forget Miss Bossy Boots?" Nina laughed.

Nina had no idea that Jordan had been snooping around her flat, looking in her knickers drawer, admiring all of her designer goods, noticing client cards and another mobile phone charging behind a pile of books on her bedside table and she was totally unaware that she had gone through her diary and had noticed she had reduced her working hours.

Aaron had told Nina to wear something sharp and sexy as he was cooking her a meal at his place and then taking her Salsa dancing. Happy with the arrangements she got ready. It was an opportunity to clarify what they both wanted from each other. As she sat on the edge of her bed oiling her skin with baby oil, Franks words crossed her mind; "I can provide you with all of that and more, with sincerity."

She didn't want Frank. He wasn't the kind of guy she would naturally go for. He was to old for her and to square. He lived the high life which was nice but Nina was grounded and down to earth, she liked a bit of everything. She liked to do mad crazy things and have spontaneous fun without being labelled childish and silly. She couldn't imagine being ladylike all the time. She liked to wear big baggy bed t-shirts and joggers occasionally, to lounge around and have lazy days. She couldn't do that with Frank unless she wore a fresh designer night slip with a pair of Prada heels to bed.

Nina applied her caramel, Lancome lip-gloss, replied to her client messages, grabbed her clutch bag and headed to Aarons apartment.

JORDAN.

Driving back home Jordan tried to figure out what Nina was up to. Part time work? How was she going to manage financially? Designer clothes, shoes and underwear? From who? She couldn't afford them. Two phones? And who were all these guys she was keeping appointments with?

Pulling up on her drive next to Marks car she smiled happy that he was back home. She rushed inside to be greeted by the sweet aroma of cooking. She walked into the dining room to a beautifully decorated candle lit table.

"Hey baby, just in time." He said pulling out a chair for her to sit. "Nice flowers."

Jordan felt a little weak, "Oh . . . erm . . . I forgot to tell you, Alec and Antoine sent them to thank us for looking after them the weekend and . . ."

"That's nice." He cut her off. "How are they getting on?"

Jordan told him the basics then changed the topic of conversation. She didn't fancy talking about Alec and his brother over a romantic meal with her husband.

After dinner Jordan and Mark shared a bath with rose petals and oils before heading into the bedroom to make sweet love all night. Mark had never loved Jordan how he did that night (she felt) he touched her in all the right places satisfying her desires, it all felt so good, she wanted it to last forever.

NINA.

"Hey sexy lady." Aaron said opening his front door to Nina planting a kiss on her cheek. "Welcome to my humble home." He said gesturing for her to enter.

He took her jacket and hung it up on a peg in the hallway.

"Shoes off?" Nina asked politely.

"No, I like watching how sexy your legs look as you walk in them." He grinned licking his lips, his eyes sparkling.

"Do you ever stop?" Nina teased him secretly enjoying his jokes and frolicking.

Nina was impressed with his home. For a bachelor pad it was clean and tidy and the décor was the Ikea minimalist look.

She admired his sense of dress and style to. She was feeling him more each time they met whether she wanted to believe it or not she was falling for him.

Aaron had cooked them sauté potatoes, salmon with parsley sauce and green beans. Nina ate every last scrap of food on her plate. "Mmmmhmmm!" She moaned smacking her lips.

Aaron chuckled at her, he loved her healthy appetite.

"Very nice indeed." She complimented him. "Thank you, I feel spoilt."

"It's my pleasure." He said standing up ready to clear the plates.

Nina helped him into the kitchen. "Leave them in the sink I'll wash them up in the morning, we got to go and get our groove on baby." He laughed spinning her around and pressing himself up close to her so their lips were just about touching. He looked deep into her eyes.

Nina decided to go in for the kill and just say what was on her mind.

"Aaron, tell me what you want from me?"

"I want you just as you are." He simply stated gazing into her eyes. "The question is Nina, what is it that you want for yourself? I believe it's time for you to be true to yourself and make up your mind what you want in life and not just from another person. I don't want to be the one to pressure you or suffocate you. I just want to make you happy but only if you will allow me to."

Nina was taken aback. Aaron was right and that was the reason she liked spending time with him. He reasoned instead of arguing or coming across judgmental. She didn't want him to back away and she couldn't settle for being just friends with him, she liked him too much to accept that. But she would be a hypocrite, he wanted all of her and with her lifestyle that wouldn't be the case. He was everything she had ever wanted in a partner, handsome, hardworking, he was the blah, bah, blah . . . the problem was her secret life. I'll stop after six months, she told herself, that way I'll be able to assess if we are stable as a couple. (She tried to justify the term; probation period.)

"Well?" Aaron asked holding her face in his hands.

"I'm a busy woman Aaron as you know, but yes I want to be with you. Could we take it slow and enjoy the quality time we spend together regardless of how often it may be? It's just that I'm a woman who has had time to appreciate her own space and company so I'll need time to adapt."

"That works for me beautiful." He kissed her gently biting on her bottom lip.

They caught a taxi to the Salsa club in Erdington and danced the night away. The crowd was a decent amount, some professionals and others out for a good time. They really enjoyed themselves.

"My car's at your's and I'm a little bit tipsy." Nina remembered flopping in Aaron's arms.

"Well you'll just have to stop at my place tonight." Aaron told her catching her.

Nina slapped him playfully, "You planned that Mr." She told him.

Aaron grabbed her tightly, "I'd love for you to stay over but if you don't want to I'll put you in a taxi home and drop your car off to you tomorrow if you'd prefer, I didn't do it on purpose I just never thought." He admitted truthfully.

As Aaron and Nina left the club and walked to their taxi Nina spotted Frank with another lady on his arm. Trying not to get jealous she smiled subtly and got into the taxi. Frank noticed her and her company also and did the same.

It was at that point Nina realised being an escort was just a job. Claire's words fluttered around her head, " . . . just sex and money, no attachments."

So what was Franks spiel all about then? Nina thought to herself.

"Did you see that?" Aaron asked. "Even that guy with his lady on his arm couldn't help but look at you." He innocently laughed beaming proudly.

13

JORDAN.

J ORDAN FILLED MARK in on the plans for Nina's birthday surprise over breakfast. She planned on cooking a three course meal for Nina, herself, Mark and 'Hazel eyes'.

"So, what's Aaron like?" Mark asked Jordan over breakfast.

"That's just it baby, I haven't actually been introduced to him properly so I thought this would be a great opportunity to see what is so special about him. He's clearly making her question certain things in her life. You know she's thinking of studying again? Fancy that at her age? Little Miss Busy Body!" Jordan replied twisting her neck. Really Jordan was holding this dinner to satisfy her curiosity.

"What's that supposed to mean?" Mark enquired picking up on his wife's expressive attitude.

"She's hiding things Mark . . ." Jordan enlightened Mark on her findings at Nina's flat the other day missing out the crucial fact that she purposely snooped about. Instead she based It all on accidental discoveries.

As usual Mark remained neutral, he refused to get involved in women's politics.

"Maybe she just wants to better herself and branch out, get out there and experience more and be part of more now she hitting the big three zero. Why can't you be happy for her and support her? She's your best friend." Mark stated bluntly.

Jordan always felt as if Mark was against her. He always spoke highly of Nina as if really she was the woman he wished he had married instead of her. Then he wondered why she felt as if she couldn't confide in him. That's the last time I tell him anything, she told herself knowing in the back of her mind it wouldn't be.

"I am happy for her." Jordan snapped bitterly.

"Yeh right!" Mark gawped laughing out loud, "Of course you are babe." He kissed her on her forehead and headed out the door for work.

Jordan wasn't far behind him.

Of late Jordan was finding it hard to face work. It was a huge and constant reminder of her cheating, lying ways as well as the daily pretence of a life she lead as if nothing had happened. In fact she wondered how she had managed it for the past how long? It didn't help that Mark was so horny lately and every attempt she made to put him off failed and each time they made love she saw Alec's piercing gray eyes reminding her of her sin.

Her days seemed to drag on forever but when home time arrived she wished it was the beginning of the day once again so she didn't have to go home and play pretend with Mark and live with the tightening knots of guilt inside of her stomach. She had considered doing an activity such as badminton or aerobics to avoid it all. But she knew she couldn't hide from the reality. She would have to face the music eventually.

Jordan sat at her desk eating a tuna sandwich and checking her Blackberry messages. Mark had text her asking if she had caught the Postman that morning. She never thought nothing of it, maybe he was excited about yet another new gadget he may have ordered on line. Nina had also text her a family of smiley faces which indicated birthday excitement. She smiled to herself for the first time that day.

"Hi Miss . . ."

Jordan looked up to see Leon (Alec's best friend) standing in front of her desk. Jordan was so engrossed in checking her messages she hadn't even heard him enter the classroom.

"How can I help you?" Jordan asked him. Her heart started beating a little bit faster as she became paranoid at what Leon possibly knew about herself and Alec. Best friends talk, what was she supposed to think?

"Alec said to let you know he will be sitting his exams and could you send his work to him through me?"

"Erm . . . yes, yes . . . that's fine, not a problem." Jordan stammered putting together some papers from the previous lesson. She handed them to Leon. "I'll set up some lesson drafts so you can help him understand a bit more, any problems just let me know. It's good that he has you to look out for him."

"He's my best friend." Leon confirmed, "I'm sure he'd do the same for me."

"I'm sure he would." Jordan agreed as Leon made his way to the door.

"Oh Miss . . ." He turned around slowly catching Jordan's eyes.

Jordan's heart started up again as she looked at him anticipating what was coming next.

"Alec really admires you and aims to make you proud. He said you really encourage and inspire him. He wanted me to let you know that." Leon said shrugging his shoulders as if to say, 'well I was just doing as I was told.'

NINA.

Nina felt all giddy inside, all the plans she had made to change her life had fallen in to place nicely. She felt contented as she made her way to work that morning full of beans. All day she pranced around the office as if she was in 'The Sound Of Music.' She couldn't stop thinking about Aaron and felt at ease that he was happy to start a slow moving relationship with no pressure and Frank had proven to her that being an Escort was just the job she thought it to be in the first place. "The woman who was clinging to his arm that night was just a replacement for me." She told herself.

Nina was also excited about the week drawing to an end as it was her birthday weekend and celebrations were to take place. She was a little bit nervous about introducing Aaron to Mark and Jordan, they were the family she had chosen and loved dearly, therefore their opinions of him mattered.

Nina met Claire at the same Café on the Bear wood high street that they had first ever meeting. It seemed like only yesterday. This meeting was arranged by Nina to discuss Frank.

It had been a while since Nina had last seen Claire and they embraced in a hug. Claire looked fresh as usual, demanding authority with her sophisticated style.

"So tell me the problem gorgeous, or should I say problems?" Claire cut straight to the point.

Nina took a ravenous bite of her tuna and mayo baguette cutting her mouth on the crusty bread, moaning in pain, and attempted to tell Claire the facts concerning Frank between bloody mouthfuls.

Claire listened attentively sipping her coffee and handing Nina handfuls of napkins. The story was nothing new to her, plenty of Escorts she knew of went through the same thing. How to handle it was the tricky part. Frank paid Nina well, showered her with gifts and even worked around her, accommodating her as if he was her Escort. The question was, why didn't Nina want him? All Escorts had at least one client who wanted them to pack it in and just belong to them entirely. Some accepted it and lived grand lives. In her eyes Frank sounded like a good catch but Claire sensed something else was affecting Nina's choices.

"Somebody else is in the picture aren't they?" Claire asked.

Nina stopped munching on her food and looked up at Claire. She failed to realise how Claire always knew something that she hadn't yet been told.

Nina then had to confess about Aaron and explained to Claire how hard she had tried to fight the feelings she had towards him, how she tried to distance herself due to her lifestyle and the new changes she had decided to make.

"Do you think Aaron is a wise move? How are you handling Aaron and being an Escort together?"

Nina wanted to cry but held it back. Had she made a mistake?

"Well, from what you tell me you seem to handle Frank quite firmly and strict, maintain that, that's good. Make shorter appointments with him and sometimes become unavailable even if you are in bed with a book, pretend you have another client appointment. As for Aaron you know it is going to be really hard. Personally I would let it go but we are two different people. You are going to have to be on your guard and be very careful so as not to leave any crumbs that could lead a trail of suspicion. I understand your line of thinking with the probation period thing as any relationship has one whether it is made apparent or not, but if he passes are you going to give up being an Escort? If so you cannot get attached to the money, or be sensible with the money you're making in the meantime so you have some for your future. You have to be sensible Nina, I must admit it's a bit of a messy situation, you have temporised your job as an Escort."

Driving back to work after her lunch break Nina was left with even more to think about. Claire was an expert Escort and Nina knew she was right and that she had to be careful. The world was too small. She hadn't told Claire about Frank and Mr Allen being cousins as Claire didn't know Nina worked for Mr Allen who was her client. Nina laughed, knowing Claire she knew who Frank was anyway.

That evening after work Nina returned home to find a massive bouquet of flowers at her door from Aaron. The card read; Thank you for a lovely weekend I hope we indulge in many more xxx

Feeling spoilt she rang him to show him how delighted she was.

"Hey baby." He answered. Nina could tell he was smiling even without seeing his face.

"I just wanted to thank you for my flower garden." She laughed.

"You're welcome."

They had a little 'chit chat' before Nina settled down to watch her TV soaps and eat some dinner. She felt all relaxed knowing tomorrow was her day off. She had no client appointments booked for that evening so she decided to surprise Aaron. She jumped into the shower and spruced up smelling eatable. She put on her Victoria Secrets set and her Prada heels with a touch of her Lancome lip-gloss. She tied her Mack on tight, got in her Mini and made her way to Aarons place. As she drove she felt pleased with herself. She had to do things like this for him to minimise the risk of suspicion and to show she could spend quality time and spoil him as much as he spoilt her.

Aaron opened his front door grinning like a Cheshire cat surprised by Nina's presence.

"What do I owe this pleasure?" He asked licking his lips as he noticed her heels and bare legs. Aaron had been chilling in front of the TV himself. "Can I take your coat?" He stared at her trying to work out what she was up to.

"Of course." Nina smiled trying to contain herself.

As she removed her coat she revealed her barely covered body and Aarons jaw dropped open as her coat slid out of his hand and fell to the floor. Leaving it on the floor, more interested in the sweetness that stood before him, he scooped her body up into his arms and carried her into the kitchen, lifting her up and gently placing her on the counter top.

"You're a naughty girl, look what you've done to me." He said looking down at his jogging bottoms rising.

Nina giggled, she loved his sense of humour. "If I never had that affect on you I would be worried."

Aaron looked at her intensely, they hadn't yet became intimate to the point of sex since they had met. He wanted her so badly right now and what made it easier was knowing the feeling was mutual.

They spent all night exploring each others minds and bodies until Aaron realised the time.

"Baby, what have you done to me? I have work tomorrow, well in a few hours." He giggled. "What about you?"

Nina didn't work Tuesdays as of now. "No, on Tuesdays I do a course as part of work so I don't start until a little later." She lied

"So you're going to stay here with me tonight?" He pleaded biting on her bottom lip and staring at her, his hazel eyes glinting.

"If you want me to." She agreed.

"I'd love for you to stay, waking up next to you may cause me to miss work though." He told her biting her bottom lip once again.

14

JORDAN.

JORDAN HAD DECIDED to busy herself with work regardless of what Mark thought of her doing so. She also took up Squash after work twice a week with Sandra, one of her work colleagues as Nina couldn't commit to a routine. Jordan was very tempted to ask her why, especially now she was part time at work, but then it would become obvious she had snooped through her diary. She also took more pride in her appearance and socialised a little more with the other friends she had instead of relying upon Nina all the time. It seemed that was what Nina was doing so she decided to take a leaf out of her book and do the same. She convinced herself that making all these changes would free her from her depressive state and encourage Mark to love and respect her a little more. Maybe if she did more things with her time she would have more to talk about and share with Mark and Nina and their relationships would blossom. After all, life could be only what she made it.

It was Thursday, the week had flown by and Nina's birthday meal was tomorrow so Jordan decided to pop into town after work and get some things in preparation. She also had an appointment to get her hair and nails done as she wanted to look and feel at her best. Mark had offered to accompany her but she refused, she wanted some time to herself.

Time got away with Jordan as usual and it was 8pm when she eventually made it home. Mark was in the office doing some paperwork.

"Hey baby!" He shouted to her as he heard her key in the door.

"Hey!" She shouted back carrying the bags into the kitchen to unpack.

She put the radio on and sang along to Boys II Men's, 'Well runs dry.'

Mark entered the kitchen and started singing along to as he stood behind Jordan clasping his hands around her waist and swaying slowly as he usually did.

She smiled, "How do you expect me to unpack if you're holding me so tight?"

Mark let her go and as she closed the fridge he placed a picture on the door securing it with a magnet.

"What's that?" Jordan asked.

"Antoine drew it for us, it came in the post this morning, isn't that nice of him?"

All of a sudden she became hot but tried to disguise it. The slightest reminder of Alec made her feel sick. Antoine had really had an affect on Mark it seemed, whether Mark wanted to admit it or not.

"Oh . . . erm . . . that's nice"

"Yes it is, he wrote us a letter to let us know how he's doing. I suppose I have a soft spot for him out of pity. I sent him a goody bag from us both, he'll be going home soon as his moms doing really well." Mark ranted on.

"That's good." Jordan pretended to be interested.

"I thought you would be pleased, it's more your business than mine." Mark stated matter-of-factly.

"What's that supposed to mean?" Jordan raised her voice and started slamming things down hard on the counter top, angry that Mark was throwing things back in her face.

"Forget it." Mark said going back into the office and slamming the door behind him fed up of having to deal with Jordan's mood swings.

NINA.

Thursday already and Nina couldn't stop smiling to herself everyday had felt like her birthday lately.

She had left Aarons on Tuesday morning feeling all refreshed and brand new. Once she returned home she was greeted by a load of client requests due to a blanket text message she had sent them all, informing them of her new schedule. She wanted this, hence the part time hours at Mr Allen's enabling it all to be possible so she just had to get on with it, there was money to be made for her future prospects.

On Wednesday evening she had a brief appointment with Frank at his office, she maintained her usual self but she detected a little bitterness on his part about seeing her the other night with Aaron. The way he thrust at her hard, fast and silently, instead of his usual soft and sensual manner made his feelings quite clear.

Aaron called Nina that evening inviting her to attend bowling with himself and his two nephews.

"I have my nephews this evening babes and they've been through a lot lately, I don't get to spend much time with them so I thought we could do something nice together. I wondered if you would like to equal the numbers and get competitive with two teams of two at bowling, what do you say?"

Nina laughed, she didn't have any plans for the evening so why not?

Aaron arrived outside Nina's flat at 6pm prompt. They greeted each other with a peck on the lips and Aaron introduced her to his two nephews who were in the back seat before they drove to the AMC Bowl Plex.

Aarons little nephew was really clingy to his big brother and so they decided to play the boys verses Nina and Aaron. The boys were in the lead to start with until Nina developed a good wrist action and hit strike after strike impressing Aaron and the boys.

"You pretended you couldn't play at first to trick us!" The youngest nephew laughed, "I want to be on your team!" He begged.

"I think he likes you." Aaron grinned.

"I like him to, he's cute." Nina smiled.

"What about me? I thought I was cute?" Aaron said pretending to be jealous.

"Green doesn't suit you Mr." Nina played with him.

Aaron and Nina deliberately let the boys win before taking them to Frankie and Benny's to eat burgers and fries. Nina watched how Aaron cared for the boys as if they were his own and was intrigued as to what the situation was with them and why he never really got to spend time with them, but she decided not to pry, the evening was flowing nicely and she didn't want to spoil it. She stared at the boys and admired their jet black curly hairs and piercing gray eyes. It seemed Aarons family had special eyes.

They dropped the boys off first and Nina didn't understand as to why they lived in separate places. To Nina they looked like children's homes and hostels.

They reached Nina's and Aaron leaned over towards her for a kiss. She kissed him back. They both sat in Aarons car for while 'chit chatting' and flirting with each other going over the evening they had spent together along with the fun and enjoyment.

Nina couldn't help herself and queried Aarons relationship with his nephews and he informed her they were his brothers children. His brother was in prison serving time for robbery and their mother didn't like them associating with his side of the family.

Nina felt bad for enquiring as she stared at Aarons sad face. She could tell he loved those two boys very much and would do anything for them.

"So how did you get back in touch with them?" Nina asked hoping for a more positive, response.

"Alec rang me and explained that their mom isn't very well at the moment hence their living arrangements. I just thought to spend some time with them today would be a distraction and remind them both that they do have someone they can come to and who does really care for them. I love those boys as if they were my own Nina and I would never want anybody to hurt them." Aaron explained.

"Do not forget I shall be picking you up at half past six tomorrow evening for the birthday meal at Jordan and Mark's, so dress to impress." She reminded him trying to lighten the mood by giving him something to look forward to. She could sense he didn't want to dwell on the subject of the boys anymore then he had already.

"Anything for my lady, thank you for coming bowling tonight it meant a lot to me." Aaron told her.

"You're welcome." Nina assured him before stepping out of the car.

After a candlelit bath Nina retired to her bed with a hot chocolate and her book when her work phone beeped. It was Frank, somehow he knew it was her birthday on the weekend. Only Mr Allen could have told him that, Nina thought to herself not knowing whether to be angry or not. When Nina didn't reply Frank decided to call. He wanted an appointment with her on Saturday evening. Nina wasn't silly she knew Frank out of all her clients would be the one to set up a birthday surprise all in vain to try and gain her heart. She tried to remind herself it was just business and that money had to be made, but the guilt kicked in when she thought about Aaron. What was she doing? "Buck up!" She told herself, Aaron doesn't have to know.

"I'll confirm it tomorrow once I know my plans for the weekend." She told Frank before closing her eyes and drifting off to sleep.

15

NINA.

NINA ARRIVED AT work to find the entire office decorated with 30th birthday banners and balloons. On her desk was a neatly arranged pile of birthday presents from her work colleagues and Mr Allen. The whole team screamed, "HAPPY BIRTHDAY!!!" to her as she entered the office that morning. Nina was baffled and surprised. Usually birthdays weren't this extravagant at work in the six years she had worked there.

"So what's the occasion?" Nina laughed sarcastically with embarrassment.

"Becoming thirty." One clever clogs remarked.

"Becoming a mature, well grounded woman of thirty." Another colleague added.

"Saying goodbye to fun and frolicking and hello to your future." Commented another.

One at a time her colleagues expressed their views on what becoming thirty years of age meant whilst Mr Allen poured everyone a glass of Shloer before finishing off with a comment of his own.

"Becoming thirty is the thirtieth reason to continue loving and living life more than when you were twenty-nine years of age."

Everybody clapped and cheered, shouting another 'Happy Birthday' to Nina clinking their glasses together

Nina resided to her office with a permanent grin on her face, she felt so happy. 12:30 arrived very soon as Nina gathered up her gifts and thanked her colleagues and Mr Allen for a wonderful morning and birthday celebration. She signed out of work and began loading her belongings into the boot of her car when her work phone beeped. It was a voice message off Frank asking if she would be kind enough to pass by his restaurant for 2pm. She laughed to herself, it was obvious he had something up his sleeve.

Before heading off to meet Frank Nina fixed herself up in her rear-view mirror, sprayed a couple of squirts of her Prada perfume and touching up her red Chanel lipstick, all the while trying to figure out what Frank had planned.

"I'll just have to go and find out." She told herself. "After all he is my best client in the sense that he pays very well. The least I owe him is my presence even if just for a couple of hours."

With that Nina made her way to the Jewellery Quarter parking on a side road.

Strolling into the restaurant trying to keep her cool and retain her nerves, Nina was greeted by a waiter at the reception.

"Hello you must be Sunshine?"

Puzzled as to how he knew who she was, she smiled politely and replied, "Yes that's correct."

"The manager is expecting you, follow me and I'll show you to your table."

Nina followed the waiter as he escorted her to a table located in the VIP section, decorated with a dozen red roses and gold stars scattered all over the table cloth. The waiter pulled a chair out for Nina to take a seat and then informed her he would be back shortly with some Champagne.

Two minutes later Frank appeared with the Champagne instead of the waiter pouring her a glass whilst holding her gaze.

"Frank?" Nina managed to mutter.

"Happy birthday Sunshine, and yes before you say anything my cousin kind of let it slip that it was your birthday as he was discussing a surprise

109

for you, which I expect you have already enjoyed this morning? I do apologise if I made you feel uneasy but the fact is, you serve me well and I do, without doubt adore you so I wanted to express my appreciation by having a birthday lunch with you. Would you grant me that?" He pleaded.

Nina couldn't refuse as she was already present and so they spent the afternoon eating and discussing life at thirty years of age. Nina felt calm and comfortable, just like the date they had at TGI Friday's, but although the case she did not feel for him like he felt for her. He was her client. Nothing more and nothing less.

Once they had finished eating Frank led Nina to his office.

"Sunshine, I didn't invite you here to conduct an appointment, it's your birthday and I wanted to give you a gift." He said handing her an envelope.

Nina slowly opened the envelope to find two tickets, all inclusive to the Maldives, departing in a weeks time. She looked up at Frank already sure of what was coming next.

"How about it? Me and you?" He confirmed, turning her blue sky grey.

She tried to think fast. She didn't want to hurt his feelings or come up with a lame excuse so as not to go. Who wouldn't want to go to the Maldives? The problem was going with him. Thoughts ran through her mind like a herd of Wilder Beast in a stampede running for their lives from a predator.

Frank was her predator.

"Frank . . . I . . . er . . . I don't know what to say. It's short notice and I won't be able to get the time off work and . . ." That was the best she could come up with.

Frank interrupted her, "Don't worry about work, take it as unpaid leave, I'll pay you for the days you miss if it's an issue." He lifted her chin and looked deeply into her eyes, "come on Sunshine, I thought you would like this?"

Nina stepped back a little and Franks hands slipped from her face.

"Frank it's an extremely kind gesture but unfortunately I can't accept this. I'm sorry." She apologised handing him back the envelope. Frank looked devastated and distraught but in the back of her mind Nina knew it would only take him a minute or two to find a replacement for her absence. Trying to avoid eye contact with him and lighten the blow, Nina kissed him gently on the cheek and thanked him once again for a beautiful birthday lunch and the roses.

Turning to leave Frank's office Nina was shocked as Frank grabbed her roughly by the arm, nearly pulling it out of it's socket causing her to fall to the floor. He then dragged her up just before she fell on her knees and threw her on to his office couch winding her causing her to gasp for air.

"Frank! What are you doing?!" She managed to holler as loud as she possibly could hoping someone might hear her and come to her rescue.

Frank ignored her and pinned her down using his weight at full force, digging his knee into her thighs.

"Please Frank, what do you want from me? You're hurting me!" Nina screamed terrified. She never thought Frank would ever treat her this way. Her eyes darted around the room rapidly as she tried to spot something to aid her survival but it was no use he had her pinned down tightly.

"I want you Sunshine and you keep knocking me back. Do you know how that feels? DO YOU!!!" He shouted millimetres away from her face, showering her with saliva. "What do I have to do to show you my love? Tell me?"

Nina had no choice but to turn on the water works. She allowed a tear to roll down her cheek. If he cared for her why would he want to hurt her? His weight was pressing down on her and his grip was so tight she saw bruises forming on her arms right before her very eyes.

At the sight of her tears Frank released his grip and got up off of her. He backed away from the couch turning his back on Nina as she furiously fixed herself up, wiping her tear stained face and frantically grabbing her belongings so she could hurry up and get the hell out of there.

"Sunshine I'm so sorry, please forgive me, I don't know what came over me, I never meant to hurt you." He turned to face her preparing to comfort her with a hug.

Nina quickly turned away from him and left the office slamming the door behind her. She made her way to the ladies room to sort herself out before heading home. She could not allow anyone to see her in such a state. She splashed some cold water on to her face to reduce the red splotches and then locked herself inside a cubicle and began counting to twenty in order to calm herself down. Really she wanted to run wailing through the restaurant like a mad woman, tainting Franks name, but then she would only expose herself. She quietly questioned herself, is this the messy part of being an Escort? She cried silently inside. Her thoughts trailed longer than a train track. She wanted her now grey sky to turn back to blue.

Glancing at her watch it read 4pm and Nina had loads to sort out before picking Aaron up for her birthday meal at Jordan's. She made her way out of the ladies and the restaurant. As she left, the waiter who had greeted her wished her a happy birthday. She plastered a fake smile across her face and thanked him. If only he knew.

Collecting her mail from her mailbox Nina entered her flat and locked the door. She sat on her bed and opened the few birthday cards she had received from friends and family before falling into a heap and stuffing her face into her mountain of pillows to stifle the sounds of her bawling her heart out.

"No crying on your birthday you'll have an unlucky year." She heard her Aunts voice in her head. With that Nina got up and ran a shower. She had a birthday meal to attend and good people to mingle with.

"I'm outside baby, are you ready?" Nina sat in her car outside Aarons place on the phone to him.

"I am but come on up I want to give you your gift." He told her.

Really Nina couldn't be bothered to make her way inside she felt battered and tired but she knew she had to perk up to dull any suspicions, so she quirked herself up, put her game face on and got out of her car.

Aaron opened his front door licking his lips as usual, indicating that he wanted a kiss. Nina obliged and Aaron squeezed her tightly.

"Ouch!" Nina winced as Aaron applied pressure to the places where Frank had hurt and bruised her.

"What's up baby? Did I hurt you?"

"Oh . . . erm . . . no, I mean I banged myself on the cabinet at work today and it's bruised and tender, that's all." She lied. "You just happened to touch that spot, it's ok though." She rambled on trying to reassure him. Little did she know Aaron wasn't buying any of it but as it was her birthday he let it slide for the time being.

"Well I didn't mean to hurt you, especially on your birthday."

Aaron led her into the living room and handed her a card and a small jewellery box.

"Thank you." Nina said kissing him softly on his lips all excited.

"Well open it then." He told her hovering over her and fidgeting like a kid that needed the bathroom.

"Ok, ok, ok!" Nina laughed at him.

As Nina opened the box she panicked and her heart began to race. It was a ring. She stared at Aaron waiting for him to take the ring out of the box and get down on one knee and propose. She stood still waiting, and waiting and waiting some more but he never moved.

"Well?" He questioned.

"Well . . . erm . . . thank you it's beautiful." She said placing it on her middle finger, right hand.

Aaron started laughing. "It's ok baby, I never meant to scare you, you should have seen your face, what a picture! It's just a ring to show you how much I care for you and to let you know you can trust me and rely on me in times of need. I don't know you entirely but I love the Nina I have had the privilege of getting to know so far."

Nina was stuck for words. After the day she had had she felt like she was on an emotional rollercoaster ride that had been around so many times she couldn't distinguish if she was up or down.

Aaron stared into her eyes looking for a sign of some sort, but instead Nina fell into his arms begging for a long, hard hug.

Aaron surrendered and held her rubbing her back and kissing her forehead.

Something wasn't right with his lady.

JORDAN.

Jordan felt like she had excelled herself in preparing the evening for Nina's Birthday. Not only was it a gift to Nina but also proof of her capabilities to be a good friend and wife, she wasn't just a school teacher. Little did she know Mark was quite aware of the few changes she had made of late but he decided to keep quiet just to see how long it lasted in case it was another phase she was going through.

The doorbell rang and Mark went and greeted the guests as Jordan finished preparing the drinks in the kitchen before skipping to the door to join them.

"Happy Birthday!" They wailed at Nina embracing her.

"Thank you." Nina smiled trying to bear the pain from her bruises which again Aaron noticed.

"You must be Aaron?" Mark said shaking his hand firmly and welcoming him inside. "Or 'hazel eyes' to the ladies." Mark added laughing.

For the first time Nina saw Aaron blush and she couldn't help but laugh.

Everyone was made comfortable and drinks served as they settled in the living room. Conversation began as Jordan was eager to discover what qualities Aaron had that had her best friend hooked. She didn't waste time firing round after round of questions checking to see if he fitted her suitability criteria all of which Aaron handled with care. He knew her game and wasn't about to slip. Mark observed in awe, he had to give it to Aaron, he was a pro. Mark liked him, hardworking, ambitious, polite, manner able and simply laid back.

Jordan had made her famous Butternut squash soup to start and had laid it all out in the dining room ready before seating her guests.

Nina wailed with pure delight as she noticed the beautifully decorated dining room. Balloons and banners in a black and gold theme. Everyone came bounding into the room to see what all the noise was about and started laughing once they realised what it was.

"It's not everyday my best friend turns the big three zero. Stop being a soppy git and lets all eat!" Jordan ordered.

They all took a seat and began their starter. Aaron felt really comfortable and Mark was pleased that for once Jordan was calm and melancholy.

"So what have you done to celebrate your birthday so far?" Jordan asked.

Nina told them all about the office party that Mr Allen and her colleagues had thrown for her that day at work. Jordan was well impressed as she knew how much of a stiff Mr Allen was.

"Mr Allen's loosened up a lot lately." Jordan commented. "What with the works do the other week and now a birthday party?"

Nina laughed. "I did notice a change in his behaviour myself actually but I've decided to enjoy it whilst it lasts."

"I couldn't agree more." Mark butted in. "Wise decision Nina. It makes the working environment a much more pleasant one."

They all clinked their glasses. Jordan more half heartedly as she wondered why Mark was always so damn perfect.

Aaron insisted he collect the empty soup bowls and take them into the kitchen to help Jordan out. He then helped her dish out the main and they each carried two plates each through to the dining room. Grateful for his help she gave him an extra helping of Macaroni cheese which Mark noticed.

"I knew I should have helped!" Mark laughed. "You know the game Aaron you did that on purpose."

"Don't hate participate." Aaron laughed back.

Both men seemed full of banter and Nina found it comforting that Aaron was so easily accepted.

Jordan couldn't help but smile as silence came over everyone bar the smacking of lips as they all enjoyed their food.

"What did Mr man here get you for your birthday?" Jordan asked Nina indirectly which Mark thought to be quite rude.

Nina knew she was trying to put Aaron in the spotlight, comparing him to Mark financially maybe. She placed her cutlery down and held out her right hand and showed off her glinting ring. "Beautiful isn't it?"

Jordan's face turned green with envy but she couldn't just leave it at that. "Oh it's on your right hand, not your wedding finger."

"That's right Jordan. Well spotted." Nina said sarcastically, patronising her. If she wanted to play the fool she would be treated like one.

"So it's just a ring then?" Jordan continued.

"No. Not just any ring. It's a ring that Aaron got for me as a birthday gift." Nina simply stated.

Aaron picked up on the vibe and kissed Nina's cheek deliberately to rub salt in Jordan's wound.

"Well I think it's nice. Well done man." Mark complimented.

They all sensed how ridiculous Jordan felt and Nina changed the subject so as not to torment her any further. It wasn't worth it.

"Mark you would be so proud if me." Nina began.

"Why?" Mark said intrigued.

"We went bowling and I was a pro. Strike after strike!" Nina said full of excitement.

"Yeh right!" Mark laughed out loud.

"Ask Aaron."

Aaron confirmed that Nina was telling the truth wondering why it was a big ordeal. He then couldn't stop laughing as he learnt about the times Mark, Jordan and Nina had gone bowling and not only did Nina perform badly but she went down the alley along with the bowling ball.

116

"Nina can't bowl to save her life!" Mark was killing himself laughing at this point causing everyone else to. "You must have some influence over her bowling skills." Mark told Aaron.

"I think it was my nephews." He replied.

"We went bowling on Thursday," Nina informed the table, "Myself, Aaron and his two nephews Alec and Antoine. They're so lovely, Antoine wanted to be on my team as I'm the 'bestest' bowler." Nina said proudly in a kiddie voice.

Mark and Jordan looked at each other astounded. Obviously due to their profession and confidentiality they were automatically restricted with the information they were able to disclose. It was a little bit too late as Aaron and Nina had already picked up by their facial expressions that something was wrong.

"What's wrong?" Nina asked.

"Alec, gray eyes and jet black curly hair?" Jordan asked describing him.

"Yes that's correct do you know him?" Aaron asked.

Jordan plastered a fake smile across her face all the time aware of Marks hard gaze warning her to tread carefully. "Yes, he's a star pupil of mine. He's doing really well."

"That's good to know with all he's going through lately." Aaron added with relief.

Although fully aware of what was going on with the boys Jordan played dumb and Mark kept quiet.

"Small world hey?" Jordan said getting up and clearing the plates.

Jordan escaped to the bathroom and threw up. She felt uncomfortable with the situation of Aaron being in the same circle as Alec. She should have guessed from the eyes. It was to close to home, to close for comfort. She was scared her dirty secret would be revealed then her life would be a total mess. If Nina continued seeing Aaron things were sure to get out of control the more familiar they became.

The others were in the living room when Jordan returned. Mark told Aaron and Nina to get comfy while Jordan and himself cleaned up the kitchen. "We'll have desert and then it's prezzies!" He laughed, "We won't be long."

Nina snuggled up to Aaron with her full stomach on Mark and Jordan's couch. Aaron decided to probe a little further concerning her bruises.

"So are you going to tell me how you really got those bruises?"

Nina looked up at him a bit upset that he was still prying, especially on her birthday. She was fragile enough but he wasn't to know that was he?

"I told you." She said.

"Yes you did Nina but there is more than one bruise, you have them on your wrists to. My concern is that someone has hurt you. I don't want to be that man that is not there to defend and protect his woman. I want you to be able to confide in me and feel safe and secure."

"I understand, but as I said . . ."

Aaron stared at her hard. He knew she wasn't going to confess so he decided to let it go. He didn't want to upset her on her birthday he loved seeing her happy.

"Ok." He left it at that.

Nina felt rubbish for having to lie to Aaron, rubbish for putting herself in that predicament with Frank and rubbish for having a secret life at that precise moment.

Mark and Jordan came prancing into the living room with envelopes. Jordan had got Nina a voucher for Vivienne Westwood shoes worth £300. Nina's eyes glowed like hot coals as she screamed in delight.

Mark and Aaron thought it was hilarious how girls went giddy over shoes.

"I couldn't believe when I saw Nina's Prada shoes." Aaron told Mark.

"The devil wears Prada!" Mark joked.

"Stop it man you're scaring me." Aaron laughed.

"Stop taking the piss!" Nina giggled. "Obviously you'll never understand."

Mark then handed Nina an envelope containing a Spa weekend break for two in Ireland.

"Awww Mark that's so thoughtful of you." She kissed his cheek.

"Take me!" Jordan squealed.

"Well who else am I'm going to take?"

Again Jordan just couldn't help herself. "I don't know, you've been real busy lately with other people. Have you not?"

Nina started to become suspicious as to what game Jordan was playing. "Work, Aaron and my Birthday." She stated clearly.

"And college." Aaron added trying to back her up.

"College?" Jordan enquired.

Nina started to perspire, as much as Aaron thought he was helping she wished he hadn't mentioned college at all.

"It's work related a day release kind of thing, you know?" Nina tried to explain.

"Well I think that's good you said you wanted to expand your career." Mark tried to reassure her it was a positive step. He knew Jordan could be a bitch.

Nina felt like she had been put on the spot. Why was Jordan doing this to her? She could be so spiteful at times.

For the rest of the evening they all played card games and watched a film. Still Nina felt uneasy and wanted desperately to know what was going on with Jordan. Sitting across the room Jordan felt quite the same.

Eventually it was time to call it a night. They all said their 'goodnights' and 'thanks'. Mark was chuffed that he had a new buddy to chill with and Aaron was thankful for the warm welcome he had received.

"I'll call you in the week." Nina told Jordan. "Thanks again for such a lovely birthday meal and the effort you put into it, it was wonderful." She said kissing her on the cheek before following behind Aaron to the car. As they backed off the drive Nina was fuming inside. Jordan was threatening her secret life silently. She knew something, but how?

Nina dropped Aaron off home. He wanted for her to stay but she conjured up a pile of excuses ranging from being tired and not having clean underwear.

"It never stopped you before. It's your birthday babes, let me rub you down and relax you. You can sleep in one of my big T-shirts." His persuasion worked and Nina's birthday was wrapped up nicely.

16

JORDAN

IT WAS 6AM Saturday morning when Jordan sprang out of the bed and galloped at high speed into the bathroom to throw up. Mark followed her and rubbed her back sleepily.

"What's up baby?" He asked worried.

Jordan heaved and spat out the remnants into the toilet. She felt like crying. She couldn't remember the last time she had vomited, probably as a child from eating too much cake at birthday parties.

"I don't know." She moaned, then she suddenly thought. "Oh gosh the dinner last night! What if I've poisoned you all. Poor Aaron, what will he think of me? I would have ruined Nina's birthday . . ."

Little did she know she was talking on deaf ears, Mark had leaned against the towel rack at this point and was snoring.

". . . I mean, how do you feel baby?"

Jordan sat back grateful she had stopped heaving and saw Mark sleeping.

"I'm talking to you!" She shouted at him, slapping his arm to wake him up. "Maybe I should call the others and see how they are feeling."

It was the weekend and Mark was tired, he wanted so badly to be in his bed and stay there till noon.

"I'm sure they will let you know if they are feeling the same." He reassured her. "And I'm sure they wouldn't appreciate an early morning wake up call."

Jordan knew he was right and after brushing her teeth she climbed back into bed and snuggled up close to Mark.

NINA.

Nina opened her eyes to gentle kisses raining all over her face. She smiled as Aarons eyes sparkled in the morning sunlight.

"Morning sweetness, are you ok?"

"I'm fine." Nina yawned stretching long and hard in Aaron's big, baggy T-shirt.

"Are you sure?"

Not again, Nina thought to herself hoping today wasn't going to be another day of Aaron interrogating her.

"Yes I am Aaron, why?" She said quite curtly.

"Because you were crying in your sleep and shouting out for a 'Frank' to stop hurting you." He informed her tilting his head waiting for her to fill him in.

Nina was stunned let alone embarrassed. (Note to self, no more sleep over's.) At a total loss for words Nina tried to disguise the whole situation and began to laugh hysterically.

"No I was not. If that was the case why is my pillow dry?"

Aaron looked at her as if she was mad. He loved her sense of humour but this was a serious matter.

"I'm totally serious Nina. You were kicking and punching the air. I had to calm you down back into a peaceful sleep. I don't want to upset you but if something was wrong would you tell me? Has this got something to do with the bruises? And who is Frank?"

Concern was scribed all over Aaron's face and yet again Nina piled lie upon lie to flitter herself neatly out of a tight corner.

"Honestly, I was probably just having a nightmare. Jordan used to tell me all the time that I would do all kinds of crazy things in my sleep from when we were kids."

Aaron stared at her long and hard listening to her rambling on and on, wondering if she was telling the truth. He kissed her forehead and climbed over her to get out of the bed.

"I'm going to make us some breakfast."

Nina was left feeling stone cold. The incident with Frank had really shaken her up to the point where it was presenting itself in her sleep through her subconscious. She dreaded to think how Aaron must be feeling about her after the past few days, he wasn't stupid and if she didn't grasp some sort of control soon it might be to late for their relationship. She had to fix this and quick.

Trying to act as 'normal' as possible, Nina bounced into the kitchen where Aaron was preparing breakfast and starting dancing around to SWV in his big, baggy T-shirt. Although feeling slightly tense Aaron lightened up when he saw Nina smiling and being silly. She automatically had that power to make him forget about being angry or sad just with her smile.

"I think I care a little bit too much for you Miss Lady." He said squeezing her tightly around her waist and kissing her deeply.

"I think you do Mr, but I'm a big girl I can look after myself."

JORDAN.

Jordan's day wasn't getting any better as she continued to feel rubbish and fragile. To make matters worse Mark had abandoned her to go and watch football with his friends including Aaron, leaving her feeling even more sorry for herself.

She decided to ring Nina to see what her day entailed been as Aaron was with Mark and Co. but decided against it. Knowing Nina with her new, up and coming lifestyle she'd be busy partaking in a whole heap of nothingness. She tried anyway out of desperation and just as she thought she reached Nina's voicemail.

Bored out of her brains Jordan had an idea. She showered and dragged on her tracksuit.

Today she was going to play Colombo.

NINA.

It was noon when Nina arrived back home from Aarons. She had told him her week ahead would be a busy one and she would call him. Really she had a load of client appointments to keep as well as work, and then the following weekend she was off to Ireland with Jordan for her birthday Spa treat, courtesy of Mark.

She wasn't sure if she was glad that she was going to have a break away from Aaron or not. He was becoming a little to close for comfort a little to soon and it frightened her as her secret had a greater chance of being discovered.

Nina took a long, hot, deep, raspberry bubble bath then lay across her bed in nothing but her underwear as she replied to messages on her work phone, checked her e-mails on her Netbook and updated her diary. She had an appointment in an hours time so she got herself all spruced up and called a taxi.

As Nina got into the taxi she never noticed Jordan parked on the roadside, sitting in her car watching.

JORDAN.

Jordan sat in her car a short distance away from the flats that Nina lived in patiently waiting to see what Nina was up to. She gathered she was home as Jordan had spied her Mini in the parking lot, so why wasn't she available to speak to her over the phone?

Something wasn't right with Nina and Jordan wanted some evidence because it seemed Nina wasn't going to tell. Who in the hell has new found confidence overnight? Makes drastic life changes such as reducing working hours and studying again just like that? Wears designer clothes, oozes sexiness all the time and has no financial difficulties doing so?

"I'm supposed to be her best friend!" Jordan cursed.

Today was what would be labelled as D-day according to Jordan. Discovery day.

She hadn't been sitting in her car long before Nina made an appearance wearing a fitted, strapless jumpsuit and her patent leather KG heels with a patterned, fitted belt and her hair scraped up into a tight bun.

Jordan's jaw dropped. Why did Nina look as if she was going on a night out when it was only approaching 2 pm?

Nina got into the taxi carefully.

"A taxi?" Jordan breathed.

The taxi accelerated and Jordan didn't hesitate to do the same. Ten minutes later the taxi pulled up outside the Radisson Hotel in the city centre and Nina stepped out once she had paid her fare.

Jordan tried to think fast as she couldn't stop due to space, traffic and being spotted by Nina. She drove round the corner and coincidently found a car park. After parking up she ran as fast as she could into the hotel lobby hurriedly scanning her surroundings for a glimpse of Nina. It was to late. She saw the elevator doors close and Nina disappeared out of sight. Jordan stood in the middle of the lobby watching what the elevator display read to see what floor Nina would get off at.

"Can I help you madam? Are you lost?"

Jordan turned around to face a woman dressed in a nice neat Radisson uniform.

"Err . . . no I'm fine thanks."

Jordan turned back around realising she had missed the stop. "Dam!"

"Excuse me?" The lady in the uniform enquired.

Jordan quickly thought. "Could you please tell me what room number a Miss Nina Rowley is stopping in?"

"Unfortunately I cannot disclose that information to you madam I do apologise."

Miffed, Jordan stomped her way out of the hotel and headed directly across the road towards Caspian pizza. She had a sudden craving for a margarita and a large salty portion of fries. After getting her food order she sat at a window seat facing the Radisson so she could eat and keep a look out for Nina.

Stuffing food into her mouth not caring that she looked a scruff bag in her tracksuit she wondered to herself, "Nina Rowley what are you up to? What goes on in that Hotel you seem to visit frequently?"

NINA.

Nina smiled as she placed her earnings into her Marc Jacobs handbag and entered the elevator. She applied some lip gloss and sprayed some perfume before leaving the hotel and jumping into a black cab totally oblivious of Jordan running across the road in her tracksuit.

As soon as Nina got home she put her phones on to charge, made a hot chocolate, set her alarm for 11 pm and got into her pyjamas. She had a midnight appointment and wanted to get some sleep before then. She yearned for sleep she was a little exhausted.

JORDAN.

Jordan yawned as she sat once again outside of Nina's building patiently waiting for her next move. Little did she know she was in for a long wait. Nina was in slumber land without a care in the world.

Becoming impatient she contemplated on ringing Nina's buzzer and having a sneaky snoop to see if she could find anything to satisfy her suspicions. What was that little trip about today?

Jordan decided against that idea. She didn't want Nina seeing her in her food stained tracksuit definitely not in comparison to her glam attire.

Two hours later and still waiting Jordan decided to call it a day and drove home.

"This isn't over Nina." She hissed as if Nina could hear her empty threat.

17

NINA.

AFTER THE LATE night appointment that she'd had with a client, Nina got home the early hours of Sunday morning and decided to stay in bed for a bulk of the day. Tomorrow was work and after the eventful weekend she had had celebrating her birthday not to mention the incident with Frank, she aimed to be fresh and prepared physically and mentally for the week ahead. It was necessary for her to be on top of her game. Recently she had let herself slip slightly.

No sooner had she lay her head down to rest, her work phone rang out. It was Claire.

"Hello." Nina answered.

"Hello gorgeous." Claire replied all chirpy. "Sorry to bother you darling but a major event is coming up that I believe you and I could both benefit from. Do you think we could meet sometime today to discuss it?"

"Sounds all exciting just like you." Nina chirped back laughing.

"You cheeky bugger!" Claire giggled.

"You are welcome to come to mine." Nina invited, hoping Claire would say yes. She personally would prefer her to as she just wanted a lazy day.

"Err . . ." Claire began to think.

"I'll cook us some lunch?" Nina threw in as enticement.

"Sure." Claire suddenly agreed.

"Alright greedy guts, come for 2pm I'll text you my address."

Once settled Nina curled up and squeezed in a little bit more sleep before having to get up yet again.

It was just before 2pm. Nina did the final check on her flat to make sure it was neat and tidy. She took the pasta bake and garlic bread out of the oven just as her buzzer went off.

"Nina, it's me Claire." She sang.

Nina buzzed her up and greeted her at the door.

"Well come in." Nina said taking Claire's coat. "You're just in time for a hot lunch. Come through and tell me what you're drinking."

Claire followed Nina towards the kitchen admiring the neatness and originality of her flat. It smelt nice and was warm and welcoming.

"Oooh, I could get used to this. Your place has such character yet comfort, you'll find me inviting myself." Claire smiled. "My place is so empty and echoing in comparison to this."

Nina smiled all proud and began dishing out lunch.

Over lunch Claire told Nina about a party that would be held the coming Thursday at the Hilton Hotel in the city centre. "It's called a Sex Masquerade." Claire laughed. She explained the fact that it was a private party hosted by non other than the famous Martin. (The guy who held the cocktail party where Nina first met Frank.) The purpose of the party was for the Escorts such as herself and Claire to have the opportunity to make a bulk of money (obviously which Martin will get a cut of) as well as have some fun and boost their clientele. The Escorts will wear a sexy lingerie costume of their choice and most importantly a mask. It would be entirely up them if they wanted to cover their whole face or not. Martin wanted elegant and sexy. He wanted it to be like a ball. A half naked ball.

"Sounds all exciting, I can't wait!" Nina grinned. "What about the clients?"

Claire told her how each Escort sends invites to their clients and allows them to invite a couple of their friends to boost the clientele.

"We won't be recognised due to our masks and we are forbidden to speak so it makes it all the more mysterious and secretive. So what do you say?"

"Definitely, if you are going to be there then so am I." Nina agreed with no hesitation.

"Good because I wouldn't miss it for the world." Claire assured her, handing her a set of invitations to hand out to her clients. "If you are not scheduled to see some of your clients before Thursday, send them a text with the password to confirm at the door." Claire told her.

The ladies shared ideas for costumes for the Thursday night Masquerade.

Nina considered asking Mr Allen for the Friday morning off as she only worked half day on Friday's. If he wouldn't allow it she was sure she could manage to plough through after a late night.

Claire recommended a decent place Nina could purchase a mask from as she gathered up her things getting ready to leave.

"Thank you for a wonderful afternoon and a tantalising luncheon in your beautiful home, next time you should come to mine."

"Claire, before you go . . ." Nina started before breaking down.

Claire looked at Nina startled by the quiver in her voice noticing that Nina was in tears.

"Hey, hey . . . stop that." Claire told her grabbing her by the hand and leading her back into the living room so she could calm down. "What's this all about?" She questioned. "We were on cloud nine a moment ago."

Nina told Claire about the incident with Frank on her birthday.

Yet again Claire wasn't surprised in the slightest. In all of her years of being an Escort she had encountered situations just like this if not worse and she herself had had to fight for survival a couple of times to.

"You're upset because you have to keep that part of your life a big secret and you have no-one to vent to and express your feelings to with ease and comfort. You handled the situation well but remember you can call me anytime." Claire reassured her hugging and kissing her forehead. "You're a trooper because you still continue being Sunshine and Nina with the same confidence and grace. Don't ever let other people bring you down. It is time to tell Frank your service is no longer available."

After more words of comfort and encouragement from Claire, they said their farewells and Claire reminded Nina about the bodyguard's number in case of an emergency and to use it.

"Send the guard a text to make him aware of your location and the duration of the appointment and if he doesn't receive a text confirming you are finished and safe he'll be there right away."

Nina felt better. Claire was right, she had held it in all week and although Aaron was concerned he was the last person she could confide in regarding her Escorting problems. Imagine that?

Nina was grateful for Claire.

JORDAN.

For the second morning in a row Jordan ran at the speed of lightening to the bathroom to throw up. She rinsed out her mouth and went into the kitchen to make a peppermint tea before curling up on the sofa with a blanket and falling back to sleep.

"Hey babes, I'm off to the gym and the sauna, do you want to join me?" Mark asked Jordan.

"Oh no thanks, I'm still feeling a little sensitive and I have work tomorrow so I'm going to relax today. Thanks anyway."

"The sauna might be good for you." Mark tried to motivate her a little.

"I said no!" Jordan snapped.

Mark just looked at her. "See you later Miss Crocodile."

Mark went to the gym and Jordan spent the day lounging around in her pyjamas. Only later that afternoon did she decide to get up and cook a big Sunday dinner.

"Mmm . . . . roast potatoes, Yorkshire puddings, chicken, sprouts, broccoli, gravy . . ." She told herself dreaming about how it was going to taste and licking her lips.

18

NINA.

AFTER AN EARLY night and near enough twelve hours of quality sleep, Nina drove wide eyed to work that Monday morning smiling. She had decided to adapt a different, more simple approach to her situation after speaking to Claire. Work at Mr Allen's was fine and would remain work, Sunshine was work also and nothing more but another job that she had to be very careful with and Aaron was her boyfriend who made her very happy. Her hardest task was keeping Sunshine separate and away from everybody. Aaron and Jordan especially. She also had to grow a thicker skin in order to handle all the trials and tribulations that came along with her secret life.

Nina reached work and had a hefty workload and she wanted to get stuck right in, she grabbed a cappuccino from the works Kenco machine and took refuge in her office to solely concentrate. Her priority was a couple of files to complete for Mr Allen by noon.

Surprised by herself Nina glanced at her watch to find it was touching 11am and she had completed Mr Allen's files. The plan was to do a bulk of her workload throughout her working week so minimal was left for Friday morning as she knew she would be working at snails pace after attending the Masquerade Ball. Smiling to herself with excitement at the thought of the Masquerade, she neatly prepared the files and made her way into Mr Allen's office. As Nina approached his desk she noticed another man sitting on the edge of the desk deep in conversation with Mr Allen, his back to her.

Mr Allen noticed Nina.

"Oh speak of the devil."

Nina didn't understand why Mr Allen passed such a comment until the man sitting on the edge of the desk turned around to acknowledge her. Her facial expression changed instantly and the colour drained from her face.

"Are you ok?" Mr Allen asked concerned, noticing the colour drain from Nina's face.

Nina stood as still as a statue surprised that a puddle of piss had not formed on the floor beneath her.

"Err . . . I'm fine thanks, just in need of some fresh air. Here are your latest files all up to date." She said handing them to him, her hand shaking. "I'm going on my lunch early I'll be back by noon."

"Thanks Nina." Mr Allen said puzzled.

With that she scurried into her office as fast as she could and grabbed her coat and bag knowing that she would have to walk past the duo once again in order to exit the main office altogether.

"Nina!" Mr Allen called out to her.

Nina really did not want to stop, she could feel Franks eyes burning through her. Composing herself so Frank could not see the affect he was having on her, she turned in Mr Allen's direction.

"Remember Frank?"

"Yes I do, I'm sorry I didn't mean to seem rude it's just . . ." Nina hated the fact that she had to play pretend.

"There's no need to apologise, I could see you were a little peaky . . ." Frank began before Mr Allen butted in.

"Well, he has kindly offered to escort you to wherever it is you might be having lunch."

Frank nodded admittedly.

Nina felt sick at the use of the word; 'escort'. "No that won't be necessary, thanks for the offer but I'll be fine."

132

She left the building as fast as her jellied legs would carry her. She decided to walk so Frank wouldn't know her car (unless Mr Allen had told him which one was hers) and marched into a little café just off the Hagley road. She ordered some pumpkin soup and found a table by the window when her work phone rang. The display read withheld.

"Hello." She answered.

"Sunshine, it's me Frank please don't hang up!" He begged.

Nina didn't say a thing she just waited to hear what nonsense he was going to come out with.

"I know what I did to you was totally out of order but believe me it was out of my character. You have very good reason to want me out of your life but I really don't want you to do that."

Nina remained silent.

"Speak to me Sunshine, say something. I miss you."

Nina took a deep breath, she had to maintain her composure. "You left me with bruises Frank, You ruined my Birthday! Believe it or not I do have a life outside of Sunshine . . ."

"I know, I know and like I said I can't apologise enough. What do I need to do to make it up to you?"

"Leave me alone. I mean it! Do not call again otherwise I will have no choice but to take matters into my own hands. I do have security."

Frank was stunned. "Are you threatening me?"

"No Frank, it's a promise, I will not have you ruining my life."

"After all I have done for you?"

"I worked for you Frank. It was a job!" Nina said becoming agitated that he actually had the nerve to look for stuff to throw back at her. She was now fuming and trying her best not to cry. Being in public helped her keep it inside.

As they continued to speak on the phone she stared out of the café window only to spot him walking down the street looking around as if he was trying to locate her. She quickly turned her back to the window.

"Ok Sunshine, or should I call you Nina? Mr Allen is my cousin and you cannot stop me going to see him." With that he hung up.

He disappeared out of sight leaving Nina on edge. Her soup no longer seemed appetising and her mood had plummeted to the ground from this morning. Just as she was about to leave the café her work phone beeped. It was a text message from Frank.

'You look amazing every time. Just thinking about the things we got up to makes me want you more. I'm sorry. Enjoy the rest of your day.'

Nina felt sick from nerves. Nervous as to what Frank had up his sleeve, although she didn't know him, she wasn't stupid.

Once back at work and no sign of Frank, Nina felt a little relieved until she reached her office to find a bunch of flowers and a box of chocolates on her desk. Just as she was about to read the attached card Mr Allen came bounding into her office.

"Nina they're from Frank, he really likes you. He remembers you from the works do, you do remember him don't you?" He babbled saving her from wasting her time reading the card.

Nina had to nip this in the bud before it spiralled out of control. Frank was using Mr Allen to get to her. She was going to use Mr Allen to put him straight.

"Tell him I am extremely flattered by his gesture but I'm not interested as I have a boyfriend."

Mr Allen's face looked surprised.

"What's with the face? Is it a shock that I have a boyfriend?"

"No. Not at all, an attractive lady like you deserves someone to treat her well. I'll be sure to tell Frank so as not to cause any complications."

"Thank you." Nina said with a massive, plastic smile plastered across her face.

"Not a problem although if given the chance I'm sure Frank would have treated you like a queen. Oh well such is life, I hope it all works out well for you."

"I'm sure he would have . . . not!" Nina said out loud once she was sure the coast was clear and Mr Allen was gone.

Nina just realised that letting Frank know she was attached was not a wise move. He was now going to do everything in his power to expose her and destroy her relationship. Damn!

As soon as Nina arrived home that evening she dashed the flowers and the chocolates in the outside bin shed and slumped in front of the television with some pasta bake she found in the fridge from the previous day.

Her personal phone rang, it was Jordan.

"Hello, how are you?" Nina asked her.

"I'm fine thanks for asking, eventually." Jordan snapped.

Nina didn't say anything for a brief moment sensing that Jordan was not her usual self.

"What's your problem?" Nina refused to pussy foot around her any longer.

"Nothing, why?"

"Because all you have done for probably the past couple of weeks or so is speak to me with total sarcasm, humiliation and attitude. Do not patronise me or assume anything about my life that you clearly know nothing about. Just be the friend that you are supposed to be and come right out and ask what you want to know! I've watched you throw your pathetic, jealousy tantrums lately. What are you jealous of Jordan? What is it you want to ask?"

Jordan didn't answer she was astounded at how Nina was going on with no signs of heeding.

"Is it the adjustments that I have made to my life? Yes Aaron makes me happy, yes I've decided to study again (she lied) and yes I have a social life, but I also make time for you Jordan. So what is it? Spit it out?"

"Ok, ok! I'm sorry don't get your knickers in a twist!" Jordan shouted before breaking down into tears, embarrassed that her behaviour had been so obvious.

Nina was fed up of her tears just because she couldn't get her own way, she had been like that forever and Nina thought it about time she grew out of it. Jordan had everything and didn't even realise it and if she wasn't

135

careful she was going to loose it all. Sometimes Nina didn't understand how Mark put up with her. In fact she was surprised they'd been married for so long.

"If you have problems Jordan you should know I am here for you. I am your friend not your competition. We are off to Ireland this weekend together remember and I want us to have a good time."

The conversation was closed on a positive note and bed seemed the safest option for Nina before she fired off another round that day.

JORDAN.

"Callum Blake! Gurpreet Singh! Louise Smith!" Jordan called her students up to her desk one by one to collect their practice exam paper results and also a revision guide. They had their exams coming up in a couple weeks and she wanted them well prepared. So far she had all confidence and faith in them as the results for their practice papers were very pleasing.

Just as she was about to go through the necessary topics to revise for the first paper, the classroom door opened and in waltzed Leon followed by Alec.

"Sorry we are late Miss." Leon apologised all embarrassed.

Alec just glanced in her direction on his way to his seat.

A few of the students in the group were surprised and happy to see Alec and started to chatter.

"Ok, ok!" Jordan said raising her voice. "Lets continue through this list. The sooner we get through it the sooner you can all catch up with Alec."

The class soon quietened down as Jordan outlined the possible topics that would crop up on the exam papers. She then explained the requirements she had concerning study leave. They had a choice of either studying at home, in the campus library or in class.

"I will be taking down the names of those who want to attend class to revise in order to make sure I am present. Whilst you revise I will have plenty of work of my own to be getting on with so revising is what I expect you to be doing. I am also willing to help out or go through specific topics a majority of you may be struggling a little with. If you choose to study at home make sure the environment is one which will allow you to do so. You are all young adults and wise enough to know you get out what you put in."

The bell rang out indicating the end of class and lunch time. The students scrambled out of the door heading for the canteen, all except Alec.

"I'll catch up with you." Alec told Leon.

"No problem." Leon nodded before rushing to catch up with the others.

Alec stood facing Jordan with her desk between them.

"Thanks for passing my work on to Leon." He calmly said.

"I'm glad you asked for it and have decided to do your exams." Jordan said, a bag of nerves.

"How have you been?" Alec asked.

Jordan stared at him trying to figure out his game. She had already been stung by him and didn't fancy it a second time.

"What business would that be of yours?" She asked abruptly.

"Because . . ."

"Because what Alec?"

"Because that time we were intimate . . ."

"What about it Alec? Why can't you just get over . . ."

Alec cut her off. "Because every time I try to explain to you that the condom broke you go off on one and I never get to finish!"

Jordan went as white as a sheet and instantly broke out into a cold sweat. She belted it out of the classroom and to the ladies. Her head started spinning and she felt weak. Suddenly it clicked. She had been feeling rough for the past few days and vomiting, especially during the morning period. In fact she had missed her period. Could I be pregnant? She thought to herself. If I am it's Marks we've been at it like rabbits lately, she tried to assure herself. She decided to purchase a couple of pregnancy tests on her way home from work.

She returned to her classroom to find Alec sat at a desk going through his revision guide.

"What are you still doing here?" She glared at him.

"I'm waiting for an answer to my question."

"Which was?"

"Come on Jordan don't play stupid."

"Do not call me Jordan, I am your teacher." Jordan was becoming impatient and uncomfortable. Alec's eyes were piercing through her more than usual.

"I remember my mom looking all peaky and pale and running off to vomit of a morning when preparing my breakfast when she was pregnant with Antoine." Alec said sarcastically.

Jordan hated him. She hated his intelligence, his wit, his arrogance, his beautiful hair and cutting eyes. She loved to hate him.

"I'm not pregnant." Jordan stated quietly full of uncertainty.

"I think you are and you just don't know it yet."

"And how do you come to that conclusion?"

"I watched you on the weekend through your kitchen window fighting to keep your breakfast down then failing to do so and getting sick down the kitchen sink. I took a chance coming to visit you but Marks car was still on the drive. Even when he had gone I stayed to watch you some more, skulking around in your pyjamas . . ."

"You what!" Jordan shivered at the thought. "I knew it! I thought I saw you a few times over the past weekends but when I looked again you weren't there. You creep! I knew it wasn't my imagination. Why were you sneaking by my home?"

"I wanted a chance to speak to you about this situation."

"Alec, even if I was pregnant it would be Marks. If you do not stay away from my private life and stop harassing me at work then . . ."

"Then what Jordan?" Alec asked standing up.

"Then . . ." Jordan didn't know what to say or do. What could she do? What a dirty, stinking mess she had fallen into.

"You will do a pregnancy test, that's what you'll do and you will tell me the results. Yes the probability of it being Marks is greater than it being mine presumably, but if it turns out to be mine I want to be part of it's life and I will fight if I have to."

"You'll have a long wait to find out."

"I'm a patient guy." Alec smiled.

He stared at her and started laughing freaking her out. She didn't understand what on earth was so funny.

"I'll see you during the week Miss. Imagine when it's born and it has gray eyes and curly hair."

"I'm not pregnant." Jordan whimpered quietly as Alec left the classroom grinning. Jordan felt like a piece of muck on the bottom of his shoes at that precise moment. She sat at her desk, clasped her hands together and prayed to God.

19

NINA.

NINA WAS EXTREMELY grateful that she now worked part time. It was Tuesday, her day off and she had a client appointment at 11am and then decided to go into town and check out the shop Claire had recommended to purchase a mask for the big night.

Nina climbed out of bed and made a healthy breakfast of fruit salad and a croissant with a cup of green tea. She was trying to be a bit more healthy as her hectic schedule left little room for a fitness regime. She was lucky to squeeze in a late night swim or a Sunday morning one.

After a long hot shower she sat on the rug in her closet figuring out what to wear. This was a new client who paid well and she had to do her best to entice him for future business. Money was on her mind as she knew more than likely she wouldn't be able to keep this life under wraps much longer and would have to give it up soon. She settled for a low cut blouse and a pencil skirt with her faithful Prada heels. She was to meet him at his work place in Erdington for office antics. Having to make a trip into town afterwards, Nina drove her car instead of taking a taxi and parked on a side road walking the rest of the way.

Knock! Knock!

"Come in."

Nina entered his office and he looked up. His name was Anthony.

"Sunshine." He smiled, standing up to greet her and closing the door.

"Hi." She smiled back walking towards him with a sexy swagger.

Anthony sat on his swivel chair and ushered her to sit on his lap. Nina did as she was instructed as he greedily undid the buttons to her blouse exposing her cleavage. She kicked off her heels and they landed by his desk as he began to suck quite hard on her breasts. Nina became a bit conscious that he may leave marks and so she fidgeted suddenly causing him to loosen his grip and kiss another part of her body, her lips.

He began making grunting noises as he tried to get enough of her all at once.

"No talking." He told her as he loosened his belt and pushed his trousers to the floor.

Knock! Knock!

They both jumped in fright.

"Are you expecting somebody?" Nina whispered, full of panic.

Anthony stopped to think who it could possibly be before he was interrupted by a voice on the other side of the door.

"Tony, it's me Aaron, I have the Audi part you requested."

"Oh shit!" Anthony said dragging his trousers back on and handing Nina her clothes, pushing her into his bathroom. "Give me one moment."

Nina's heart started pounding. She knew that voice anywhere, it was her man. She couldn't believe this, the fact that he was delivering an Audi part confirmed it as that was part of his job working for Audi. As she crouched down against the bathroom door trying to listen in on the conversation she felt sick to her stomach. This was way to close for comfort.

Anthony had opened the door eventually letting Aaron into the office.

"What took you?" she heard Aaron question.

"I was on the toilet mate." Anthony laughed.

"Well here's the part, it should fit perfectly."

"Thanks Aaron you're the man!"

"Tony, why are a pair of heels by your desk?"

Nina cringed. She prayed he didn't take a closer look because he knew her Prada heels very well. Very well indeed.

"They're Tracey's from across the hall." Anthony lied walking Aaron away from the desk to the door.

"Yeah right Tony, you're funny, I know you got a lady up in here and you were getting freaky. I'll leave you to it." He chuckled as he left.

Nina could not let on that she knew Aaron and conducted the rest of the appointment as necessary. She didn't feel comfortable but she knew she had to perform to get paid.

An hour later, glad that it was all over she made her way back to her car constantly watching her back in case Aaron was still around, her head pounding in unison with her heart. Once inside of her car she took a deep breath and rubbed her temples.

"OMG!!!!" How close was that?"

Once in town, it didn't take long for Nina to find the shop that Claire had told her about. After having a rummage she decided on a half mask that covered her eyes and nose with a thin netting that covered her lips and chin. "Ooh nice." She thought out loud. This would go nice with her netted thong and bra that exposed her nipples.

As she drove home she realised how risky her lifestyle was let alone frisky. She was doing things she would have never even dreamt of doing. She participated in acts and events that she once would have turned her nose up to or ran a mile from or even been to shy to consider attending or taking part in. But it was all so exciting and so much fun. Was it the adrenaline rush? Living on the edge? The thrill? Or was she just out for a good time, naive to the consequences and dangers that were to follow?

Nothing good lasts for long so enjoy it while it does, she told herself trying to justify it. She looked at the fat wad of cash lining her purse from just one hours work.

Nina had not long stepped inside of her flat when her buzzer went off.

"Hello." She answered through the intercom.

"Hey babes it's me." Aaron answered.

Nina buzzed him in. Her mind was all over the place, she couldn't think straight. Aaron had caught her off guard. She kicked off her Prada heels and dumped her bags in her bedroom before greeting him at the door making it out as if she had been in a while.

"What are you doing here?" She asked him as politely as she could. She was happy to see him but hated people just turning up, especially after the day she had had and due to him.

He kissed her softly on her lips as he entered, looking around suspiciously. She didn't seem right. She was acting funny, fidgeting and on edge. Her cheeks were red and the TV wasn't even on.

"You just got in?" He probed.

"Yes, long day at college." She quickly replied.

Aaron bent down to take off his Adidas and spotted her heels. It made him think about when he delivered a package to a customer earlier on in the day causing him to laugh. But as soon as he started to laugh he stopped.

"You wore your Prada heels to college?" He asked twisting up his face.

"Yes. I like to look decent everyday. Why?"

"And that you do." He told her ignoring the question and kissing her neck, sniffing it discretely at the same time for any unfamiliar scent.

Nina became a little nervous as to what Aaron would find if he continued kissing her like that near her cleavage. She hadn't had time to check herself over and so she backed away slightly.

"No baby, I've had a long day I must smell a little, I need to have a shower, You get comfy, I won't be long."

"Let's shower together." Aaron suggested with a cheeky grin on his face.

"No baby, I'll be quick, make me a cup of tea I'm parched." She pleaded exhausted from trying to persuade him to leave her alone.

Before he could reply Nina had locked herself in the bathroom.

Whilst Aaron waited for what seemed like an eternity for the kettle to boil, thoughts started running through his head. He looked again down the hall at Nina's Prada heels next to his kicks. They were just like the ones in Tony's office that morning. Or where they? He heard Nina singing in the shower and made his way into her office to nosey whilst waiting for the kettle to boil. On her desk he noticed a few invitation flyers for a Masquerade party taking place at the Hilton in town on Thursday. He laughed as he scanned the details, it seemed so wild. Who would attend an event like that?

"No!" He whispered.

He listened to make sure the shower was still running before making his way into Nina's bedroom. He saw loads of bags thrown in the corner and had a nosey through those also. He came across a big box and laughed, remembering what Mark had said about women and their shoes.

"Probably some extra long knee high boots." He smiled, at the thought of Nina trying to seduce him in them. As he discovered the contents of the box his smile turned into a frown. His stomach churned as he saw the mask.

Hearing the shower stop suddenly he quickly put everything back as it was, ran into the office and grabbed one of the Masquerade flyers off Nina's desk shoving it in his jeans pocket, making it back into the kitchen to continue making the tea just as Nina came out the bathroom.

"I'll just be in my room moisturising baby." She told him.

"No problem." Aaron shouted down the hall, grateful that he didn't have to look at her right away after his discoveries. If his suspicions were right he wasn't about to let her get off lightly, but to make sure, he needed evidence. Nina was his world and made him so happy, he didn't want to mess up a good thing based on assumption.

"Your tea is in the living room, I'm off, I want an early night." He told her as he tried to put his kicks on as quickly as he possibly could and get the hell out of her flat and her presence without letting on how he was feeling and why.

He felt like he was suffocating and not very good at disguising his feelings he had to leave right away.

Nina came out of her bedroom wrapped in her towel to face Aarons back as he headed out of her front door.

"Bye then." Nina said dumbfounded.

With that she put on her pyjamas and sat on her sofa drinking her ready made tea.

Meanwhile Aaron sat in his car staring at the flyer.

"Please God, please, I don't want to know what I think I know to be true, tell me another lie." He prayed.

20

NINA.

THE NEXT COUPLE of days flew by and before Nina knew it she was getting herself ready for the Grande Masquerade Ball. She'd been waxed and exfoliated to smoothness all in preparation for a good night money wise. As she perfected her costume she couldn't help but laugh at herself and the situation she was about to get herself in tonight. Although her stomach was full of butterflies she used them as fuel to ride her nerves and get her through.

"I can do this." She told herself.

Everything was prepared for work for the next day so all she had to do on return was go to bed. Grabbing her mask, slipping into her Jimmy Choos and grabbing her purse, Nina made her way downstairs to her taxi. She thought it best to place on her mask once near the venue before stepping out the taxi.

AARON.

Aaron could not concentrate that day at work and had been taken aside numerous times for the silly, careless mistakes he had made all because he was thinking about Nina and what she may be up to.

It was 8pm as he sat in his car with the engine off outside of Nina's apartment looking at the Masquerade flyer over and over as he gripped it tightly in his hand scrunching it up.

"Please Nina stay in tonight baby, for me." He begged.

To his disappointment he watched as a taxi pulled up not far in front of him and Nina strolled out of her building and climbed in. Aaron checked her out, her Mack was tied up tight, he stared at her sexy legs in heels and had a flash back to the night she surprised him by turning up at is flat in the same Mack and bare legs. He caught sight of her mask dangling from her hand as she slipped into the taxi. His heart dropped into the pit of his stomach as he fought hard to keep his emotions at bay.

He dialled her phone and to his surprise she answered.

"Hello baby, how you doing? I haven't heard from you all day are you ok?"

Aaron felt choked. "I'm ok, just had a busy day. So what are you up to tonight?" He awaited the taste of her bitter sweet lie as he watched her speaking to him on the phone in the back seat of the taxi, non the wiser of his presence and basking comfortably whilst feeding him even more lies.

"I'm going to Jordan's for the evening so I'll speak to you tomorrow as I'm about to drive off now." She lied further.

"Ok baby, have a good night and say hello to Jordan for me."

"Will do." She made kissing noises down the phone to him.

Aaron started his car and followed the taxi. His head and his heart were hurting. He had started the process of grieving for the end of his relationship because he knew it was coming, he felt it creeping up on them. The pain was excruciating.

JORDAN.

Jordan sat at the kitchen table marking mock papers and sipping on a cup of coffee to keep her awake.

Mark had unexpectedly told her he was going out with the boys for the night and didn't know what time he would be back. Since when did he go out on a Thursday night? She thought without making a fuss (because that's what he wanted her to do) and got on with what she needed to do regarding her work. In fact she was glad for her own company, he hadn't been acting his usual self around her the past couple of days and she couldn't stand it much longer.

Deep down she hoped he had a secret that would ruin everything between them, that way she wouldn't be solely responsible for when it all fell apart. She could feel it creeping up on them.

Having thought long and hard all day Jordan decided to call Nina and arrange a dinner date to tell her the truth about her situation. She really needed Nina right about now but when she rang her mobile she reached voicemail. Disheartened because she was all psyched up to tell her about her dirty secret, she put it down to fate and thought maybe she'd tell her on their trip to Ireland.

MARK

For once Mark had agreed not to be a square and go gallivanting with his boys for a night out, regardless of it being a Thursday night. Anything was better than being around Jordan, he needed to escape her foul mood swings.

"Oh my gosh! You're being a bad boy! You've broken out of jail!" Clive, one of Marks friends teased.

"Yes, but I'm not to get to drunk, just a little tipsy." Mark said laying down his rules.

"Ok." They all laughed in unison knowing that he was going home full to the brim of alcohol.

"So what's the plan?" Mark asked as he was the last to jump into the seven seated taxi.

"We are heading to the Hilton Hotel for a private party. I got us some passes to this Masquerade Ball thing that's going on." Clive told them all.

"What's that all about then hey?" Some of the guys asked excited with curiosity as Clive always organised the best nights out.

Clive explained the whole set up, the masks, the sexy ladies, the sex, drinks, money etc. Once he had finished he laughed as he looked at a bunch of guys with hanging jaws. What a result!

"Bring it on!" They all shouted with pure excitement.

"Don't worry mate, if you want satisfaction you have to pay for it, these are professionals. I know you're married dude but what goes on tonight with the boys, stays with the boys." Clive tried to reassure Mark.

"Whoop whoop!" The guys cheered. "Hell yeh!" Dazed at the thought of breasts and booty.

Mark looked glum and sad, "But what if I get tempted?"

"You can look." Clive joked, "But I'm going to have a touch and a fondle!"

Mark felt uneasy about the whole situation but if what he thought to be true regarding Jordan . . . oh well what the heck? As Clive said he was allowed have some 'eye candy.'

NINA.

Claire met Nina at the door of the venue. They had described their masks to each other for recognition purposes.

"Check you out!" Claire screamed, full of amazement. "My do you look sexy I could do you myself." She laughed causing Nina to grimace at her.

"I'm liking the full mask." Nina complimented Claire. "Oh and a whip? No messing around with you tonight!" Nina laughed even more.

"No way baby, got to make that money." Claire laughed back cracking her whip.

With that the girls made their way inside. It was traditionally decorated with heavy velvet curtains, chairs, chaise lounges and sofa's. Candles glowed on five foot tall candle stick holders and a massive chandelier hung from the centre of the ceiling. There were twelve small rooms located off the main hall and within the main hall were another twelve booths.

Already business had started taking place as guys were picking girls and vice versa. Some had already taken a few booths and rooms, while others were getting wild in the main hall performing oral sexual acts for all to see.

Escorts were not aloud to speak. They were provided with name badges. They were there to perform.

Nina looked around to see if she could spot any of her clients after Claire had already left her side and wished her a fantastic night.

After about five minutes had passed Nina spotted a couple of her clients with some of their friends but they weren't to recognise her due to her mask. She went to the bar and ordered herself a glass of pink champagne. She downed it like it was a shot and then ordered a Tia Maria with cranberry juice when she clocked Frank. Quickly she spun around on the bar stool to face the bartender who also had a mask on, but despite her efforts Frank found her.

"I know this body anywhere. The beauty spot on your side and those dimples in your lower back." He whispered into her ear brushing her earlobes with his lips and feeling on her backside.

Nina spun around to face him. She knew the rules and so did he, she wasn't allowed to speak.

He was a paying client, she couldn't refuse him, so he thought.

Security tightly surrounded the premises and also existed inside to prevent anything getting out of hand.

"So, I'm paying are you playing?" Frank asked as he went to bite her nipple peeping through the net of her bra.

She moved his hand away from her.

"Oh it's like that is it?" His face turned serious, Frank was a winner and was used to his own way. He didn't like loosing.

Nina raised her hand in the air, Frank looked confused as her rented bodyguard (courtesy of Claire) marched over and removed him from the premises, winking at Nina, reassuring her that she was now safe.

As her bodyguard finished getting rid of Frank Nina noticed a group of guys come bounding into the hall laughing and joking. They all looked quite handsome and she grinned, pound signs flashing in her eyes. She retrieved her drink off of the bar counter top and took a sip ready to attack but suddenly stopped in her tracks nearly dropping her drink. Her legs turned to jelly as she clambered on to the nearest stool, not caring about how awkward she may have looked.

"Mark!" What the hell was he doing there? Her night hadn't even begun.

MARK.

As Mark entered the venue he stood in awe and amazement at the goings on. He was tipsy and hungry for something, but he knew he had to find some self control.

Any form of restraint went to pots as he caught sight of what he thought to be the most beautiful woman in the world. His feet carried him toward her. Her thighs were thick, legs strong like a horses, skin looked so smooth he could taste it melting in his mouth, stomach flat with slight abs and a beauty spot on her side. Her mask had a net covering her mouth so he could just about make out her sexy lips.

"She's fine!" He breathed out loud getting Clive's attention.

"Go get her man." Clive prodded him.

"No, I have a wife I can't. Plus I don't have that kind of cash. That girls out of my budget I can't afford her."

"Don't worry about that, we are all going about our business so I got the bill, go ahead." Clive pushed him a little. "Don't do anything I wouldn't do." He chuckled. "Anyway, remember what Jordan's done. The pregnancy test?" Clive reminded him, trying to encourage him to get it on.

Mark stood still gazing at her. He read her name badge, Sunshine. "Two wrongs don't make a right. Ah, what the hell, one touch . . ."

NINA.

"Sexy Sunshine."

Nina turned around and came face to face with Mark.

151

"That's what your name tag says." He slurred at her, then grinned showing her his full set of teeth.

Nina stood frozen, scared that he may recognise her. She didn't know what to do, Mark was her best friends husband. He was like her best friend, a brother. This was really awkward and uncomfortable. He stood looking her up and down lustfully, reeking of alcohol. Thank God it's a Masquerade she thought not sure what was about to happen and trying to think of her escape route.

She eventually confirmed her name with a nod.

"Well you see the thing is . . ." Mark began.

"The thing is sexy Sunshine . . ." butted in another taller guy who clearly knew Mark, " . . . we are all about to get busy and my man here has been drooling over your fine ass since the moment we walked in here, so tell me the price and I'll pay for you to make him smile."

Nina shook her head. No way could she do this. Just at that precise moment Martin walked by and caught on to what was going on.

"£500 and you can have this booth right here." He saw them into the booth made sure they had their privacy by drawing the heavy, velvet curtain and hooked it closed and flipped the sign so it read occupied. "Go have some fun and enjoy." He said clapping his hands in mid air.

Mark sat himself down comfortably on the grand chair and lifted Nina up and placed her in a straddle position on his lap so she was face to face with him. He started to touch her tracing her neck with his fingers. He flicked her nipples peaking through her netted bra and began to suck on them with his warm, wet tongue. It was all to much.

"You are so amazing, I cannot believe I'm here touching you." He said kissing her stomach. "I really want to put it on you, dam you are so hot!"

Nina was grateful that she was not allowed to speak otherwise he was sure to know it was her by her voice.

Mark continued to slur at her.

"I have a wife Sunshine and the reason I have ended up here is because our marriage is on the rocks." He said placing ice cubes, along with his fingers in Nina's mouth and rubbing her breasts with another.

"There's something about you that makes me feel at home, something warm and familiar."

Nina reached to the side table to take a sip of her drink in order to calm her nerves, this was getting out of hand. Her best friends husband had her straddled on his lap and was touching her intimately.

"Anyway, as I was saying . . ." He started taking off his clothes. "I want to feel your soft skin against mine, mmm, you smell and feel so good . . ."

He reached for a condom out of the basket on the table.

Nina started to panic and got up.

"No baby, I need you, I need this. Satisfy my desire please don't leave." Mark begged her pulling her back to him.

Nina stared at Mark. She didn't want this.

"I want you to make me feel good, I want to make you feel good. There's no betrayal, you and I don't have to feel guilty at all Sunshine because my wife is pregnant . . ." He said capping his tool then lifting her up and placing her back down on top of him so fast she had no time to escape. He purred into her breast in sheer delight.

Nina couldn't think straight. That was it they were officially having sex and Jordan was pregnant? Great! Mark started panting and grunting as he gripped her tightly.

". . . but it's not my baby . . . oh gosh . . . mmhhmm . . . and I know because we've been trying for a while . . . ahhhh . . . and she never got pregnant . . . oh yes . . . ahhh . . . so I went to the hospital and guess what?"

Nina could not look at him. She felt disgusting because of what he was telling her as well as what they were doing. This was Jordan he was talking about, her best friend.

"I'm firing blanks! I couldn't get anyone pregnant if I tried so I know it's not mine . . . ahhh . . . oh gosh! It feels so good, mmm."

After a few more minutes of moaning and groaning Mark released his load and clawed her back burying his head in her breasts sucking on them once again and breathing deeply.

"That was amazing, you're beautiful and gorgeous and sexy and . . ."

Nina helped Mark clean up as he was a little slow due to being drunk and then left the booth. She bumped into Clive who was just coming to see if Mark had been satisfied and told Nina that Martin had been paid before slapping her ass. She walked away from the booth leaving Mark and Clive, she didn't want to hear the 'boy talk' as she already felt terrible and disgusted with herself. She went to the ladies to sort herself out.

The night had just begun and already she had slept with her best friends husband. How could she? She felt selfish. Really she should have revealed her identity so it never got that far but she'd rather do what she had just done then expose her own secret. What kind of person had she turned into? Not only that but she now had another secret to keep under her wing, and had also learnt about Jordan being pregnant but not for Mark. So for who? What had she been up to?

She leaned over the sink to balance herself, her hands were shaking and she felt weak and unsteady. What a dreadful mess, it seemed like everyone had secrets.

Nina realised there and then that being an Escort was more trouble than it was worth and as of now she was going to stop. She was going home and changing her life back to normal. She'd continue working three and a half days and actually go and study and maintain her happy, conscience free relationship with Aaron. Her mind was set right there and then.

She gathered her things together, texted Claire, collected her money off Martin and bid all a goodnight leaving the venue on the excuse of not feeling very well.

It was over. No more Escorting!

AARON.

Aaron leaned against his car waiting patiently in the cold night air. It was keeping him calm as he waited to spot Nina leave the Hilton. He knew he would flip if he went inside the hotel and saw all that was going on. It didn't matter how hard one tried to pretty something up, ugly was ugly. Escorting was prostitution sugar coated as far as he was concerned.

He saw her leaving, she had only been inside two hours, why was she leaving so soon? She never hailed a taxi either, to his surprise she wrapped herself up in her own arms and began walking at a fast pace slowly removing her mask.

He watched her, his angel, his world, his everything. He wondered how she was going to respond to his presence, he wondered if now was the right time. Maybe he should have gone inside the venue to see for himself but he knew his heart wouldn't be able to cope with the naked truth.

He approached her, grabbing her arm and spinning her around so they were directly face to face with each other. He noticed her name badge and frowned.

Nina gasped. "Hi baby, what you doing out here?" She asked shaking like a leaf numb from shock and the cold night air.

"Hi Sunshine, did you have fun at your dirty party?" He said shoving the flyer in her face.

"Aaron . . ."

"Don't say my name! You're a liar Nina and I never ever thought you to be that girl. I fell hard for you, but you are just a dirty slut! How could you? How could you do this to me? I would have given you the world if I could, wasn't I enough for you? Did you get bored of me?" Aaron was fuming, he was about to explode.

"Please Aaron . . . listen . . ." Nina noticed the sparkle fade from his hazel eyes and knew this was it. Nothing she could say there and then was going to save the pair. This was the end.

"No more Nina, no more! It's over." And he turned away from her making his way back to his car.

Nina started to chase him.

"Stop it! Look at you, you're pathetic. Mark once said the devil wears Prada and that's what gave you away. He was right and there was me thinking it was a joke. I made a delivery on Tuesday Nina and it was your Prada shoes sitting at the foot of my customers desk, or should I say your customer? You get around don't you? Did you ever think about me whilst you gave yourself to other men? Did you ever think about us? DID YOU?! Is it money you want? Here take it!" He shouted at her drawing attention to them both by throwing a mixture of notes and coins at her.

Nina stared at Aaron, tears filled her eyes as Aaron had his fit humiliating her in public. He then got into his car and drove off leaving her standing there totally embarrassed twisting the ring he got her for her birthday around her finger.

21

NINA.

NINA MADE HER way to work thinking about the night before and how Aaron had driven off leaving her standing alone in the middle of town. She felt exhausted from bawling her eyes out. Why was it that the moment she decided to pack it all in and do the right thing, was the moment it all fell apart.

She had tried to call Aaron numerous times but had reached his voicemail. He clearly didn't want to speak to her and who could blame him, but she really needed to talk to him and try to make him understand. She had fought hard not to become attached to Aaron, trying to convince herself that she didn't need him or want him when really she did. He had been the best thing for her and now he was gone.

Feeling tender Nina entered her works building. As she made her way through the corridor towards the main office she noticed a trail of A4 posters plastered along the walls. She stopped and took a closer look at one of them nearly stumbling to the floor when she realised that it was a photo of her wearing her Masquerade outfit. Underneath read the caption; Sunshine aka Nina, here to satisfy your desires, please call . . . and her work mobile number was printed on the poster.

Nina started to hyperventilate as she ran to the ladies only to discover more of the same posters covering the bathroom walls as well. Everyone stared and sniggered at her and some of the guys even took out their mobile phones to enter the number whilst laughing. Luckily she had left that phone at home saving herself from further embarrassment.

Locking herself in a toilet cubicle was becoming a regular occurrence. She felt ashamed and humiliated. Who would do this? Surely Aaron wouldn't stoop so low.

Having made her way through the main office brushing off the stares and sniggers, she eventually reached her office and collapsed into her chair and cried only to be distracted by the bleeping of her computer telling her she had mail. She opened the mail to find a message from Frank; 'I did you a favour and opened up a whole new clientele for you, enjoy.'

Nina dropped her head back onto her desk and continued sobbing. "I should have known."

Half of the morning had gone before Mr Allen knocked on Nina's office door. Nina had finally got a grip and accepted the fact that she was dwelling with the garbage. She had no boyfriend and an exposed dirty secret. She was dreading the finale when Jordan found out and Mark discovered Sunshine was actually her. She would then have no friends and be a renowned marriage wrecker. (Maybe not if what Mark said was true about the baby not belonging to him.)

"Nina are you ok?" Mr Allen asked her quietly slipping into her room.

"Mm." Was all she could fathom. If she tried to speak she felt she'd crumble into a million pieces.

"I've taken all the posters down and we'll forget any of this happened. Whatever you choose to do in your own time is your business, it doesn't concern any one else."

Nina couldn't believe Mr Allen was so kind about the situation. Then it clicked, he was a client of Claire's, he used an Escort, he was trying to justify his own actions indirectly, secretly thankful it was her who was exposed and not him. Nina turned to face him and he smiled happy that he now had her attention.

"This is all your fault!" She barked at him clenching her fists. "If it wasn't for you conducting your personal business in the office pretending to be carrying out interviews, I would have never have gotten into this mess!"

"Hold on a minute Nina, I don't understand why whatever choices you chose to make has anything to do with me!"

Nina didn't want to mention Claire so she skimmed the surface.

"I saw you having sex with an Escort Mr Allen and I saw how much you paid her. It seemed like an exciting, adventurous, hectic, busy, lifestyle. I was attracted to all of that and the money and being my own boss was the icing on the cake, I wanted some control over my own life that's why I went part time, it was all of that, it filled my void. I thought it made me happy . . ." Nina blubbered tears streaming from her eyes.

Mr Allen felt sorry for her. She was crying out for some stability in her life.

". . . then I met your cousin Frank and he became infatuated with me although he was just a client. He didn't like me escorting and tried to sway me to be with just him and I rejected him. It's he who has set up this poster thing . . ."

Mr Allen listened in amazement. He could not believe what he was hearing. He would have never guessed in a million years what Nina was going through, she seemed like a simple girl who lead a streamlined life.

"Listen Nina we can rectify this." He told her.

"How?" Nina asked.

"You can have your full time hours back and I will have a word with Frank. How about that?" He leaned his head to the side to try and catch her eye.

Nina was very grateful for the offer of her full time hours back but she declined them. The whole situation had made her realise that It was time to move on. Money wasn't an issue as such and she had a good enough academic background to easily get another job.

"Thank you Mr Allen but I think it's time I moved on, I'll be handing in my notice on Monday. I'm sorry."

With that said she gathered up her stuff, gave Mr Allen a hug and clocked out of work ignoring the stares and giggles from her soon to be ex-colleagues.

JORDAN.

Jordan rolled over to an empty space in the bed that her and Mark shared. He hadn't come home last night and she was angry that he hadn't even had the decency to call to let her know he was safe at least. To make matters worse, when she tried to call him she reached his voicemail.

When she got to work that morning she rang Marks school to see if he had reached work but they said he had called in sick.

"Bloody liar!" She screamed slamming her folder down on her desk causing her coffee to spill soaking some of her papers.

Set in a bad mood for the day, Jordan opened her class at 9am for those students who wanted study time and revision help. Every time the door opened she would hold her breath hoping that it wasn't Alec, she didn't have the energy to battle with him today.

Jordan pulled up onto her drive next to Marks car happy to be home and to break her pregnancy news to him. "Maybe he would stop ignoring me and things will get back to normal when he finds out he will soon be a dad," she thought. She put her key in the door to find suitcases at the bottom of the stairs and boxes full of paperwork and Marks computer.

"Baby!" She called up the stairs. "Where are you? What's going on?"

Mark came bounding down the stairs with another case. His eyes were red from alcohol overdose and lack of sleep. He glanced at her before dropping the case and heading back up the stairs to pack some more of his stuff.

Jordan was lost, she didn't have the slightest idea as to why Mark was packing. Had someone told him about her and Alec? But no one knew but her and Alec. She followed him up the stairs.

"Move!" He told her.

"What are you doing?" She asked him.

"What does it look like? I'm moving out."

"But why?"

Mark put the box down that he was holding in his hands and turned to face her. Suddenly Jordan felt a little threatened.

"Why do you think? You tell me Jordan. Tell me!" He shouted at her.

"I . . . I . . . don't know what you're going on about." She stuttered.

"You don't?" He said making a clown face at her as if she was stupid. "Well let me show you." He told her running down the stairs and retrieving some letters from one of the many boxes before running back up the stairs to where Jordan sat on the bed in their room.

"Read this!" He shouted at her causing her to flinch by shoving the letters in her face.

Jordan took the letters and read them out loud.

"So how can you be pregnant?" Mark asked her.

Jordan could not look at him. Instead she spoke directly to the floor. "How did you know I was pregnant?"

"Ahh come on Jordan, the morning sickness. It was taking so long for us to make a baby I had questioned if it was possible for us to have a family at all, ever, and I decided to go the hospital for some tests to see if it was me, I needed to be sure that I wasn't to blame for us not being able to have a family. I then found the pregnancy test sticking out of your bag reading positive when I had already received a letter telling me I'm firing blanks!"

"They could have it all wrong!" Jordan started to cry.

"So why the tears then? Shall I request another test for certainty because you are absolutely sure you're carrying my child? Shall I? And embarrass you more when they're sure I'm firing blanks and you are lying?"

"But I love you." Jordan cried.

"Oh please Jordan do not take me for fool. Tell me what I need to hear, tell me the truth."

Jordan couldn't speak, she wasn't expecting this. It was Alec's baby for sure especially now that Mark had the tests done. What a mess.

"TELL ME!!!" Mark bellowed for all the neighbours to hear.

Jordan ran off and locked herself in the bathroom. Mark packed up his car panting with anger. How could she? He kicked the bathroom door and shouted, "Wait until my mother hears about this and I will find out who that baby's father is believe me! I already felt less of a man but you have just confirmed that for me. Thanks a lot Jordan, Thanks a bunch!"

With that he grabbed the last box, got into his car and drove off leaving Jordan drowning in her pool of tears.

NINA.

Nina got home and started packing her weekend bag for her Irish Spa getaway trip that Mark had booked for her birthday. She was glad to leave the week behind. Her personal phone beeped. It was a message from Jordan apologising as she wouldn't be accompanying her to Ireland as she wasn't feeling very well.

Nina texted her back to let her know she was still going she was in need of a pamper and time out.

Nina packed the last of her things, checked that her flat was left secure and called a taxi to take her to the airport. This was the time to assess her life once again.

22

JORDAN.

J ORDAN LAY WRAPPED up in her duvet wearing her baggy pyjamas and bed socks. All that she required surrounded her bed, from tissues for her runny nose and teary eyes, to a bottle of water and munchies to satisfy her cravings. She had placed the house phone and her mobile on the bedside table just in case Mark called. She had decided to hibernate for the weekend. Her life was officially a mess. Her marriage was broken and she was carrying Alec's baby.

She rolled over to check the time on the clock and glimpsed the photograph of herself and Mark on their wedding day. She felt betrayed instantly. Why would Mark go alone to have tests concerning their ability to conceive? The both of them were supposed to be in it together, do it together, make decisions together. They were a married couple for goodness sakes and she did not recall him mentioning having any tests done to her.

More than likely he would be staying at his mothers house being her only child and a spoilt brat at that.

Nina crossed her mind. Jordan couldn't believe she had still hopped on the flight to Ireland on her own. She seemed so brave and confident, her life seemed like sweet candy and here she was wrapped up in heartache and pain, the rotten batch. Maybe I should have gone with her and pretended everything was picture perfect with my life she thought.

NINA.

Nina boarded her flight and took her seat at the window. Part of her was quite happy to be spending the weekend away from Birmingham but part of her wished she had company to share some laughs and jokes with.

She made up her mind to take full advantage of this birthday gift and indulge in the spa treatments to refresh her mind and body. She had hit the ground and she was going to use this weekend trip to help herself get up. Decisions had to be made as to where she was going from here and once she had weighed up her pros and cons she realised she had a lot going for her and it wouldn't be that hard or complicated to move on with the right approach.

Ordering a large glass of Moet just for the sake of it, she pulled out her Elle magazine and made herself as comfortable as she possibly could for the forty-five minute flight ahead.

The plane hit the runway and once her ears had popped and they were gliding through the clouds Nina's mind ran on Aaron. She really needed to speak to him and make him understand that she never intended to hurt him.

Digging her notepad out of her hand luggage she composed a simple schedule for her weekend in Ireland with a smile on her face for the first time that day.

MARK.

Mark shoved his bags and boxes in the spare room at his mothers house before flopping on the bed that his mother had just made up for him in his old room all the while attacking him for answers as to why he had showed up on her doorstep with all of his belongings.

"Not now mum!" He had shouted at her slamming his bedroom door.

Mark's mobile rang and he reluctantly turned the screen over to see who was calling. He was surprised to see that the caller ID read Aaron.

"Hey mate, what's up?" He asked.

"Hey," Aaron replied, "I was just wondering if you'd like to grab some food and a drink, I'm pissed off man, been having a crazy time of late."

Feeling exactly the same he agreed to meet Aaron at the Junction pub in Moseley Village in the next hour. Anything was better than staying at his mothers with nothing but earache.

"I'll see you shortly." Mark told Aaron.

With that Mark jumped in to the shower and dug some clothes out of one of his cases making a vow to sort it all out tomorrow.

AARON.

Aaron had just got the drinks in and the menu's when Mark arrived.

"So what's happening?" Mark asked Aaron taking off his coat and taking a sip of his drink followed by a gasp.

"I don't want to seem like a big girls blouse but I've finished with Nina and it's messing me up." Aaron admitted.

"Well, snap!" Mark laughed although clearly unhappy about it all.

"What do you mean, snap! You've finished with your wife?" Aaron enquired, flabbergasted.

Mark told Aaron the whole story, from trying for a baby, the tests and the results (regardless of the embarrassment) and then Jordan being pregnant.

"But what if the hospital were wrong and the baby is your's?" Aaron suggested.

"I'll let them carry the tests out again but Jordan didn't tell me what I needed to hear. Not once did she assure me that I was the only one, that it could only be mine. She branched out on me Aaron, she slept with someone else."

"How do you know?" Aaron asked still trying to digest it all. Jordan and Mark were a nice couple and from the first time Nina had introduced him to them and they had spent time together he placed them on a pedestal. They seemed such a strong, positive couple. But as they say, you never know what goes on behind closed doors.

"I feel it, I feel it in my heart. But I'll tell you something, I will be damned if I'm going to raise another man's child. I've been thinking until my head hurts Aaron, trying to figure out when she could have cheated on me and it falls on the time I went to Scotland for a week with my class."

Aaron didn't know what to say. If Mark was right and Jordan was a cheat no wonder Nina and Jordan were best friends. That would make them two peas in a pod.

"I'm sorry man, I hope you are wrong for the sake of your marriage and this unborn child." Aaron offered.

The two ordered some food and another round of drinks before Mark knocked on the door of Aarons problem.

"What I'm about to tell you, you can't tell anybody." Aaron warned Mark although he felt ridiculous because everybody probably knew before him.

"No problem, the same goes for what we just discussed concerning my situation." Mark laughed passively making Aaron feel more at ease.

"You know I really liked Nina, I really fell for her, fell for her hard." Aaron began.

"Yes, we noticed." Mark chuckled.

"Then I started noticing things the closer we became . . ."

"Like?" Mark said tucking into his lasagne and chips.

"I don't mean to be crude but she was freaky in the bedroom, attentive, which I thought nothing of at first, I just presumed that's my girl, I'm lucky. Then other things like her dress sense. She always dresses on point, sharp, sexy, co-ordinated not to mention expensive . . ."

"Where is this leading Aaron?" Mark asked becoming impatient trying to work out what could have possibly torn the pair apart.

Aaron pulled a crumpled flyer out of the back pocket of his jeans and placed it on the table in front of Mark.

"I found this when I went to visit her at her flat last week." He told Mark straightening out the Masquerade flyer. "As I continued snooping around, I found a mask as well."

Mark picked it up and had a look. He swallowed a chip whole and it burnt his throat as it went down. He needed to know why Aaron was showing him this before jumping to any conclusions.

"And?" Mark asked staring at Aarons sad face trying to keep calm.

"She attended that party Mark. She attended that party to work. She attended that party as an Escort by the name of Sunshine. Nina is a working Escort by the name of Sunshine and she's been sleeping with other guys whilst having a relationship . . ."

"Ok, ok, calm down and keep your voice down." Mark cut Aaron off.

Aaron told Mark the whole story from the delivery of the Audi part to Anthony and spotting Nina's Prada heels, finding the flyer and the mask, to following her and confronting her as she left the party.

"I don't believe this!" Mark said shaking his head.

"My lady was giving herself to other men with no regard for me. Knowing that she wrapped her strong, sexy legs around other men drives me insane, they felt her soft skin and kissed her luscious lips . . . she didn't belong to just me . . ." Aaron whined.

"Stop it! You'll drive yourself crazy!" Mark stated before excusing himself to go to the bathroom.

Mark splashed cold water over his face about four times before he felt cool enough to go back out to where they were sitting. He had up and left Jordan, sure she had cheated on him and now he had discovered that he had slept with Nina, his wife's best friend let alone a friend to himself and the girlfriend of his mate. He tried to look at it as he was tricked. He didn't know it was her and that was the truth, but she knew who he was because he wasn't the one wearing a mask. He wondered why she had let it reach the point of them having sexual intercourse without saying something, he wondered if Aaron had seen him at the party at some point and all of this meeting up malarkey was a trick to catch him out as well.

He started having flashbacks of that night, the drink, how he lusted long and hard after Nina. Aaron was right about her strong legs and soft skin. If Jordan ever found out she'd have something to say about how she

S. J. Brown

knew he always fancied Nina. He remembered touching and kissing her breasts, he remembered it feeling so good.

"Oh shit!" He screamed. He remembered telling her he was firing blanks and Jordan was pregnant. What if she didn't know.

It was all to late now the damage had been done.

Mark returned to the table after stopping off at the bar to get another round of drinks in, making sure his was a double.

"So what are you going to do?" Mark asked.

"I can't be with an Escort. I thought she was an angel, I thought I'd finally found the one." Aaron admitted.

"Talk to her, find out the reason as to why she did it. I've known Nina near enough my whole life and I would never believe she has always been Escorting. It must be a recent thing." Mark tried to reassure Aaron. "Give her a chance to explain."

"I can't even look at her, I was prepared to do anything for that girl. I'm not sure she's worth my time." Aaron stated.

With that the two drank up and called it a night.

23

NINA.

FEELING BRAND NEW Nina dragged her suitcase through the Arrivals at Birmingham Airport. It was early evening and she couldn't wait to get home to put her plan into action, starting with her letter of resignation for Mr Allen.

Deep in thought whilst making her way towards the line of black cabs, Nina failed to notice Mark walking alongside her calling out her name. Only when he called out her name for a third time quite loudly, did Nina snap back into reality.

"Mark, what are you doing here?" She asked, greeting him with a hug and a kiss on the cheek. She had to be polite, after all she was journeying back from an all expenses paid trip courtesy of him.

"Nina, I booked your trip remember therefore I knew your return time." He informed her as he hugged her back quickly not wanting to feel on her body for to long to prevent flashbacks.

"Did Jordan send you to pick me up? Bless her heart." Nina smiled. "How is she feeling?"

"No Nina. I came to pick you up because we really need to talk." Mark told her seriously, ignoring her enquiry regarding Jordan.

Nina picked up on his serious tone and noticed his empty eyes. Her mind began to race, jumping hurdles, trying to figure out what could have possibly drove him to the airport to collect her in order to talk. Maybe he needed to vent and tell her about Jordan being pregnant, or maybe he wanted to discuss the fact that she took the trip alone, or maybe he had found one of the posters Frank had made and clicked that he had slept with her.

"What is so important that you have come all this way to get me?" Nina asked, bracing herself.

"I know." Was all Mark replied before taking Nina's case and leading the way to where he had parked his car. He loaded her case into the boot and started the engine. Nina had not spoken at all, she was waiting for Mark to speak but nothing was said as they drove all the way to Nina's flat in silence. She thought the whole thing was totally crazy, what on earth was going on?

Mark parked up outside Nina's flats, turned the engine off and glared at her lustfully. She always looked and smelt so nice just like Aaron said, she was always smiling and happy and did what she had to do, no holding back never waiting for anybody. He liked and admired that about her and since the whole Jordan business he did think that maybe he had made the wrong choice by marrying Jordan.

"What are you doing Mark?"

"Am I making you feel uncomfortable?" He said leaning towards her. He then touched her neck tracing his fingers down towards her cleavage. "Does this remind you of something?"

Nina tried to silence her breathing and brushed his hand away from her skin. "Mark! Stop it!" She slapped his hands away.

"Why Sunshine? Thought you would be used to this, isn't it part of the job?"

Nina felt sick as she turned her face away from Mark to stare out of the window and fight back tears.

"How did you find out it was me?" She asked him still gazing out of the window. She couldn't bring herself to look at him, she felt so embarrassed and ashamed of herself.

"That's irrelevant Nina. What I want to know is why you carried out the ultimate move with me knowing full well who I was? I'm your best friends husband and your friend. I'm also a friend to your man! I had no idea who you were . . ."

"And that makes it right? That means you did not do anything wrong? What is this Mark? Do you feel guilty for having sex with me or for branching out on Jordan? I could have been anyone, would that have made a difference? You're trying to turn your guilt into blame to make yourself feel better and make me feel worse than I already do. At least I know what I have done and how I have hurt people. You and Jordan are both as bad as each other if what the alcohol encouraged you to admit is true, so why don't you go back home to her?" Nina spat at him before releasing the locks herself and clambering out of the car.

"Yes I was drunk but you weren't!" Mark tried to get her back for putting him in his place.

"Grow up!" She shouted back dragging her case and making her way into her flat.

Mark continued to follow her trail. They entered her home and she set her case down and put the kettle on.

"Listen to me Mark, I'm sorry for what I have done but I do have my reasons for doing them. I didn't want the fact that I was escorting to come out over revealing my identity to you knowing you are my best friends husband and you were in such a vicinity. Call me selfish but the outcome ended up worse then both initial reasons put together and I regret it all deeply, so deep you'll never know. I've hurt people and so I'm hurting to. Do you think I don't know what I have done? Now please Mark I have things to sort out, please leave me alone" Nina cried.

"Nina, Jordan can not know about this?" Mark begged.

Nina carried on unpacking her case when Mark grabbed her arm. "Nina are you listening to me? She mustn't know about this."

"Suits me fine Mark, do you think I want to hurt her as well? I've already hurt you and Aaron won't even breath by me." She agreed swallowing back emotions. "Does Aaron know about us?" She suddenly thought out loud.

"No he doesn't, but he really feels for you I'll tell you that much. Give him time he's just in shock." Mark informed her.

Mark told Nina everything that had happened between himself and Jordan and how he was back living with his mother until he could figure out what to do.

Nina was upset and angry that considering Jordan was supposed to be her best friend, she had been left in the dark. Even Mark questioned that to, he thought they told each other everything.

"So what are you going to do?" Mark asked Nina.

"You'll see." Was all she said as he hugged her tightly. She cried from her heart so he hugged her even tighter, no more questions. He shed a few tears himself knowing that there had to be an end to all of this somewhere, but it wasn't going to be just one end and it wasn't going to be a happy one.

"It'll all get sorted don't worry." He said kissing her forehead.

JORDAN.

Jordan hadn't heard from Mark since the day he had left taking his belongings with him. Through the entire weekend she had only got out of bed to go to the bathroom and stock up on junk foods. She had received the occasional text off of Nina letting her know what spa treatment she was indulging in, in order to make her jealous, followed by a load of, 'hope you're feeling betters.'

Jordan did wish the situation was different. That she was pregnant with Marks child and they were happy. To top it off she had to prepare to tell Nina the truth when she got back and she wasn't ready for the lecture on how she had it all and has now thrown it away.

Lying in her bed rehearsing how to tell Nina, trying to figure out what to tell and what not to tell to make it seem not all that bad, her thoughts were interrupted by the doorbell ringing.

"Who could that be?" She said as she tried to fix herself up as best as she could hoping and praying it was Mark. She quickly bolted it down the stairs to answer the door.

"What do you want?" She asked Alec as he stood at her door. He had had all his curly hair shaved off into a neat fade and his little facial hair neatly trimmed drawing more attention then before to his piercing gray eyes and making him look more mature.

"I came to check up on you, make sure your ok."

"Why would you . . ."

"Because you're carrying my child." Alec cut her off.

"How do you come to that conclusion?" She asked tilting her head to the side.

Alec laughed at her, he could see she was vulnerable and upset and decided to play on her emotions. He stepped up to her a little closer so he was right by her face.

"Because Mark has walked out on you, he hasn't been here for a couple days. He walked out on you because he found out you are pregnant but not for him and I'm guessing you haven't told him it's mine." Alec chuckled.

"Go away Alec, leave me alone and don't come back. You've got it all wrong!" She shouted after him.

"But you are carrying my child and so it has everything to do with me, as you said I'm a young adult, we both knew what we were doing when we were doing it Jordan. Why are you trying to hate me when all I have ever done is like you? You're the one making this harder than it has to be."

Jordan decided to put an end to all of it right there and then. She was sick of Alec's mind games and she knew full well she couldn't have the baby. She went in for the kill.

"There is no baby Alec, I had a miscarriage."

Alec's face dropped and he stared at her deeper then ever before.

"You're lying." He told her, you just want me to leave you alone.

"Oh come on Alec, why do you think I've been in bed all weekend unwell?"

Alec still stood staring at her. "If that's the case I'm sorry. But I just need to know, was it mine?"

"Go away Alec." She said, closing the door in his face and returning to her duvet.

24

NINA.

NINA WAS SHATTERED after her meeting with Mark and had gone to bed without typing up her letter of resignation for Mr Allen or sending a blanket text message to her clientele to inform them she would no longer be available.

"I'll have to sort it all out at work." She told herself as she drove up the Hagley Road to her office.

As usual gossip doesn't last long, something new always turns heads, which Nina was thankful for as she was no longer the topic of conversation in her work place.

Her head was feeling sensitive, not only did she have a lot to organise, she had a lot to think about and to top it off she was missing Aaron.

Mr Allen knocked on her office door around mid-morning just in time to receive Nina's resignation. As she handed him the envelope his eyes drooped and he resembled that of a lost puppy dog.

"Are you sure this is what you want?" He asked Nina.

"Mr Allen, I'm positive. Please don't worry and stay rest assured you are not the reason I'm doing this. I'm sorry for all the things I said to you the other day, I never meant it. You were absolutely right, I made my own choices. As I told you before, it's time for change." She smiled at him although her heart was broken.

"I'm so sorry it has come to this Nina, I'm really going to miss having you around and all your hard work . . ."

Nina handed him a key ring she had purchased for him from Ireland.

"You'll find someone who is just as good as me if not better." She said sympathetically.

"If I can do anything to help please let me know." Mr Allen kindly offered her.

"Actually there is." Nina laughed.

Nina clocked out of work that evening smiling. Mr Allen had granted her some of her annual leave entitlement with her resignation providing her with more time to sort herself out.

Before driving home she looked at her phone for what was possibly the hundredth time that day hoping to see a text at least from Aaron.

Nothing.

JORDAN.

Jordan had called in sick after deciding to book herself in for an abortion. It was study time for the students so all that was necessary was for the classroom to be available for them to get on with revision and help at stand by if required. She was sure that could easily be sorted out. She had bigger things to stress about. Luckily she was granted an appointment late afternoon that same day after successfully convincing them that counselling was not needed, it was a case of failed contraception.

Making her way back home that evening after her appointment Jordan felt a great sense of relief. She wasn't proud of having to go through the process but the truth was it couldn't work out or be accepted. She was no longer under Alec's watchful eye and with no baby he had no reason to harass her anymore. Now she had to worry about Mark forgiving her and coming home which she knew would be the hardest part.

As she approached her front door she stumbled upon Mark's mother sitting on her doorstep. (Sometimes she thought she may as well open up a shelter the way folk ended up on her doorstep)

"So you are still carrying on as if nothing has happened?" She stabbed at Jordan.

"Life goes on and Mark has made it quite clear that he no longer wants anything to do with me, so what am I supposed to do?" Jordan asked her putting her key in her front door.

"So is it true that you are pregnant for another man?" Mark's mother stared at her coldly awaiting confirmation that Mark's accusation was correct.

"Yes I was but am no longer due to a miscarriage. Now is there anything In particular you came all this way for?" Jordan said sarcastically about to enter her home.

"I got what I came for thank you very much, no need for me to come in. You are a dirty, unfaithful slag of a woman, I knew my son was to good for you!"

"Oh, before you go, just to enlighten you, I wasn't the reason we couldn't get pregnant obviously, your so-called perfect son isn't as perfect as you believe him to be, so I suggest you take care of home before you go around watching and judging others." And with that Jordan slammed her front door.

Feeling sickly and weak, not wanting Nina to even suspect what she had done today she called her to reschedule for the next day as they were both off work. She then crawled beneath her duvet and bawled her eyes out.

25

NINA.

NINA WAS UP early the next morning, she had a busy day ahead of her. First on her agenda was to pay a visit to Jordan and catch up on all that had been going on concerning Mark and the pregnancy. Really Nina was intrigued to who the baby was for, she was totally astonished that Jordan had even had an affair, it seemed so out of character for her.

Later on she then had a dinner date to attend with Claire to spill the beans and explain the fact that she would be taking early retirement from escorting. Nina laughed to herself as she brushed her teeth, knowing Claire she probably already knew what was on the cards already.

Scanning her closet rails for something comfortable yet presentable to wear, she heard her personal phone beep.

"Alright Mrs Punctual, I'm coming." She said to nobody in particular presuming it was Jordan texting her with her impatient self.

Eventually ready and good to go, Nina grabbed her coat, bag and phone and left her flat. Once inside of her car she read the text message she had received. Taking a look at the name that flashed across the screen made Nina stop for a brief moment and take a deep breath. Aaron had eventually text her, 'I need to understand, make me understand.' Nina was in total shock, she felt numb. She never thought he wanted to know her or even communicate with her, she thought she meant nothing to him, she believed she was now a ghost.

As she made her way to Jordan's house she drove with a slight glimmer of hope in her heart. Knowing she had inflicted a hurting upon Aaron made it apparent that they could never be what they once were but to at least be civil to each other would be something at least.

Nina arrived at Jordan's just as her mushroom and cheese omelette was leaving the frying pan and becoming well adjusted on her plate.

Having felt like she hadn't seen Jordan for a long time, she kicked off her shoes, dropped her bag at the foot of the stairs and embraced Jordan tightly as Jordan did the same. They stood for ages squeezing the life out of each other, it was now their time.

Over breakfast Jordan told Nina her story about what had happened with one of her students and how they had become quite close when Mark was away in Scotland on a school trip. She refused to mention the students name convincing Nina that it was irrelevant when really she knew Nina knew of him and wouldn't be able to handle her reaction. She expressed how lonely she was at the time due to Mark treating her like a baby making machine.

"I felt like a piece of meat, no affection, care or sensuality, nothing. I craved attention and unfortunately received it from the wrong person. I should have known better but I was weak and couldn't fight the feeling . . ." Jordan rambled on trying to justify her actions with reasons she believed to be concrete.

Nina didn't say a word. How could she after the things she had done. At least Jordan hadn't slept with Aaron. Or had she? Was the baby his? Who knew and who cared? It would only be what she deserved, what with herself and Mark doing the do. Jordan had no idea and Nina prayed it would remain that way, that was one secret she wanted to take with her to the grave.

JORDAN.

"Nina?" Jordan stared at her feeling uncomfortable dwelling in the silence.

"Yes Jordan?" Nina replied escaping her daydream and staring back at Jordan indicating she had been paying attention.

"Why aren't you lecturing me? Why aren't you telling me how I've messed up? That I'm pathetic and silly because I had it all . . ."

"Because I don't have to Jordan, you know that already. We are both grown women, totally aware of our actions and responsible for the decisions and choices we make. What's the point in blaming, fighting and regretting it all, the damage has been done and the fire ignited."

As Nina spoke she noticed tears roll down Jordan's cheeks as she listened intently.

"We're only human Jordan, we're allowed to make mistakes, we all do, nobody is perfect and especially not me, therefore who am I to lecture you or judge you? I understand how you felt, lonely, empty, craving and yearning a loving touch and I'm sorry I wasn't there for you. The fact is I was chasing after other things, things I thought were important, that would make me happy and whole, provide me with excitement, fulfilment, happiness and contentment when really it exposed me to pain, betrayal and placed me right back at square one . . . empty and lonely."

Jordan stared at Nina without the foggiest idea as to what she was talking about.

"I was mistaken like you. I had it all and I lost it due to the foolish choices I made. I lived in a fantasy world with all the fluffy clouds misting my vision so I was unable to see clearly, unable to see that all I ever needed and all that was good for me was right in front of my face."

Nina cried long and hard whilst Jordan rubbed her shoulders crying also at the sight of her best friend breaking down.

"I don't understand." Jordan told Nina in hope of finding out what it was that Nina had done that could have been so bad.

Nina couldn't bring herself to tell Jordan her dirty secret, there was already a truck load of pain circulating amongst her little family.

She swallowed hard, "You do understand Jordan, you just have no idea what I have done. All you need to know is that I have learnt from my mistake and I need to move on and leave it all behind because I cannot fix it back to what it was initially. Aaron and I are no longer an item because of me and I have left my job. Jordan, I've decided to go to America and stay with my brother for a couple of months to get myself together. Who knows I may end up getting a job out there and having a life."

"No!" Jordan shouted at her, "I need you, don't leave me, you are all I have left!"

Nina felt cold and good for nothing. "You and the baby can come and see me for holidays . . ."

"There is no baby!" Jordan screamed holding on to Nina drenching her with her tears. "I lost it."

Nina cradled Jordan in her arms and together they cleansed their aching souls. Tears of sadness, guilt and pain flowed from their swollen tear ducts.

"I have nothing left Nina. Mark won't talk to me or breath by me. He wants a divorce, half of the house, he despises me and I cannot blame him, but if he had cut me a bit of slack and respected me for the person I am then . . ."

Suddenly it came to Nina.

"Come with me. Come with me to America we can start again. What do you say?"

26

AARON.

Aaron had returned home that evening after going to the pub with Mark for a bit of time wasting and distraction to find Alec, his nephew on his doorstep.

"What's up Alec? What are you doing here?" He asked him full of concern.

"Nothing's wrong, I have my exams coming up this week and I wondered if I could stay here with you for the week to do my revision? I don't fancy being alone"

Aaron pushed his nephew playfully. "Sure you can, I could do with the company it would make a nice change. At least then I can keep a watchful eye over you."

They both laughed as Aaron picked up Alec's back pack and showed him inside.

As Aaron made up a bed for Alec they both engaged in conversation.

"Where are you just getting home from?" Alec asked, slurping his coke through a straw.

"From the pub with my mate Mark." Aaron told him shaking the pillow into it's case.

Alec stared at his uncle as he continued making up the bed. He was wondering if it was the same Mark he was thinking of.

"Mark? You've never mentioned him before." Alec questioned as if he was his uncles girlfriend with raging suspicion.

"Oh, he's a good guy. Do you remember Nina?" Aaron asked him trying to familiarise him by making a connection.

"Yes sure, she's your girlfriend right?"

"Well, her best friend Jordan is . . . well . . . yes married to Mark. They held a birthday party for Nina not long ago and I met them there and since then Marks become a good friend."

Alec didn't utter a word, he placed his can of Coke on the bedside table and helped his uncle finish making up his bed. He felt really awkward and realised how small the world actually was. Not wanting his uncle to latch on to his silence he decided to break it and enquired a little more about Nina.

"How is Nina?"

"We're good." Aaron lied. He didn't want to involve his nephew in his private affairs, what was going on between him and Nina was their business and he already had Mark to confide in so to involve anybody else would be unnecessary.

"Is she coming round this week? I hope I'm not going to be in the way." Alec queried.

"We are both really busy this week so I'll probably see her on the weekend. If you was in the way I would have sent you back home." Aaron laughed.

"Cool, thanks for letting me stay." Alec grinned.

"I have work in the morning so here are a set of keys." Aaron handed Alec the spare set of keys. "Make sure you revise and when I get home we'll go out to eat or something."

"That'll be great. Goodnight uncle."

"Goodnight Alec."

That night as Aaron lay in bed he thought about Nina. Mark had tried to encourage him to talk to her and try to understand why she did what she did.

Having Alec come around and discuss her brought back the memories of all the fun times they had together. When he first noticed her in the night club dancing away in her element, how she loved food but was so trim, her beautiful smile and cheeky laugh. Damn he missed her. He missed her like a well misses water and like the sky misses the birds.

Speaking to her was a big no right about now his wounds were still fresh.

Aaron then wondered about his nephew and what the real reason for his presence was. He'd find that out tomorrow when they would go out to eat.

Before he closed his eyes to sleep he went through his phone looking at the photos of him and Nina. He could still smell her scent on his t-shirt.

NINA.

Nina was yearning for her bed, her haven. She had just got home after her dinner date with Claire. Just as Nina had guessed, Claire knew what was coming and therefore was not surprised in the slightest.

"Don't you think that's a bit of a drastic decision to make so soon?" Claire questioned Nina after hearing her plans o move to America.

Nina convinced her she was certain and that it was just for a couple of months to get her head together.

"You will love it over there and then you won't come back!" Claire said panicking that she'd loose her friend.

"Well you will just have to come over to America and cause havoc then!" Nina bantered with her.

As they made their way back to their cars Claire grabbed Nina's hand.

"I'm so sorry how this has all turned out, I feel as if I'm to blame for everything." Claire said sadly.

"No!" Nina assured her. "Never. I made those choices so don't you dare go blaming yourself. Some things are out of our control and Aarons presence in my life was one of them. Things happen for a reason."

Nina stood astonished. For the first time ever she saw Claire's eyes fill to the brim with tears as she let them spill and fall on to her coat collar. Nina wiped her tears away for her with her hand straining to holding her own tears back.

"I'll call you." She told Claire.

"You better." Claire sniffled back at her. "Oh and Nina?" Claire called back to her.

"Yes?" Nina replied.

"Make Aaron understand through a letter."

That night Nina lay in her bed and just as Claire suggested, put pen to paper.

JORDAN.

Jordan lay in her big, empty, king sized bed considering Nina's proposal to go to America.

What did she have to loose? What was there to stay for? If Nina was going which she seemed very adamant about, then she would really have no one.

She was sick of moping around her house and had decided to go back to work just in time for the first set of exams. She had to face the music sometime whether Alec was present or not, he was no longer a threat to her.

That was it, Jordan had her mind set, she just had to prepare her letter of resignation and let Mark have the responsibility of selling the house as she was going away. He could keep her updated via e-mail.

Trying to drift off to sleep Jordan found it hard from trying to figure out what Nina had done that was so bad causing her and Aaron to split. It seemed such a shame, Aaron was so good for her.

27

AARON.

"How did you get on with your revision?" Aaron asked Alec over Nando's.

It had been a long day for Aaron but he did promise to take Alec out to eat so he had taken him to the Nando's on Broad street.

"Yep, I'm ready for my first exam tomorrow." He told his uncle.

"That's good to hear Mr confident." Aaron said sarcastically.

As they ate, Aaron couldn't help but stare and admire at how much Alec had grown up and developed into a young man. He felt a little sad that due to certain circumstances he had missed out on being there for him and Antoine how he would have liked to have been.

"What are you thinking about uncle?" Alec asked taking a big bite of his pitta.

Aaron finished chewing the food that was in his mouth and looked at Alec. "I was thinking about you and how I haven't really been there for you as much as I would like to have been."

Alec could see the dismay in his uncles eyes. "That wasn't your fault. You have been more of a father to Antoine and me than our own. You're here right now when I need you aren't you?" Alec grinned tilting his head at his uncle.

"Remember that I am here for you both, no matter what it is I'm here, do you understand?" Aaron reinforced.

Alec avoided answering and took another bite of his pitta.

"Well?"

"Well what?" Alec nervously laughed.

"I'm not stupid Alec, I know something has been going on with you, so now is the time to talk to me about it."

"Not here and not now uncle." Alec told him. "This is the popular Nando's and I don't want anyone overhearing my business, I'll tell you when we get home."

"Fine." Aaron accepted. "Eat up then."

An hour later Aaron sat rubbing his head in awe and amazement as his nephew told him that he had slept with one of his teachers when her husband was away. He also learnt that it resulted in her becoming pregnant for him due to the condom bursting. Her husband found out and had left her.

As Aaron listened intently the story sounded all to familiar and it began to fit into place. Suddenly it clicked.

"Is her name Jordan?" Aaron asked Alec.

"How do you know that?" Alec asked turning bright red.

"I can't believe this. Back in my day we had crushes on our teachers but for goodness sakes Alec!"

Alec ignored his uncle and asked him again, "How do you know her?"

"Because Jordan is Nina's best friend and my mate Mark is Jordan's now ex-husband." Aaron ranted, ashamed and confused. He certainly wasn't expecting to hear anything like this. "Do you have any idea what the two of them are going through right about now? Do you know the consequences of your actions?"

"It takes two uncle." Alec tried to shun the blame.

"That makes you clever does it?" Aaron patronised him full of disgust more so as it was so close to home.

Aaron was fuming, he would never have thought it to be his nephew to cause such grief and destruction to other peoples lives especially after all the things he'd had to contend with growing up. Marks words circulated around his mind, 'I refuse to raise another mans child!' And, 'I will find out who the father is.'

Alec sat, ears open, waiting for his uncle to fire more lectures at him but they didn't come. Aaron fell silent.

"I really liked her uncle, she inspired me to do well with my studies, she was there for me, it just happened." Alec tried to explain all in one go.

"They are good people Alec . . ." Aaron began.

"I know they are." Alec agreed before telling his uncle about the Bank holiday weekend when Mark and Jordan helped him out with Antoine whilst he went on a hunt for his missing mother.

Aarons jaw dropped. "Is there anything else you haven't told me? Why didn't you come to me Alec? Or was that a ploy to get a little bit closer to her?"

A tear rolled down Alec's cheek. For the first time he couldn't pass off his careless actions. For the first time he realised the trouble he had caused, not just to an individual but a few people. The knock on affect and connections were made apparent to him by his uncle and the reality had set in. He had been a brute. He felt pathetic and could now understand why Jordan despised him.

Aaron watched his nephew cry. It was all well and fine being angry at him but what was that going to solve? The damage had already been done. The last thing he wanted was for Mark to find out that Alec was the father, God knows what he would do. He put it down to the challenges his nephew had come up against causing vulnerability to be a weakness that required a helping hand and Jordan's hand was the offered help.

Aaron hugged Alec tightly and allowed him to free the tears that had been in shackles for the longest time and cleanse his soul.

"It's ok Alec, I won't tell, we'll sort this out, don't worry."

"Alec continued crying, "She lost the baby, she had a miscarriage."

Aaron looked up at the ceiling still holding his nephew and silently thanked the Lord.

"Listen, go and have a shower and I'll make you a hot drink, then get to bed and get some rest you have your first exam tomorrow and I want you prepared. Put all of this behind you for now, your main priority is to concentrate on your future. If you see Jordan you speak to her only if you have to, do you hear?" Aaron instructed him.

"Sure." Alec replied.

"Oh Alec, I'll drop you off at college tomorrow on my way to work."

"Thanks uncle."

Alec started up the shower and Aaron went into the kitchen and put the kettle on and found some mail that Alec must have left on the side for him. One of the letters looked a little odd in a flowery envelope. There was a scent on the envelope, a familiar scent . . . Nina. He opened up the letter and began to read it as he waited for the kettle to boil.

Dear Aaron,

I wasn't quite sure how to make you understand why I chose to do what I did but I'll give it my best shot.

I can assure you first and foremost that my intentions were never to hurt you, I will have to go back to the beginning in order to make you realise this.

I was bored of my mundane routine, non-existent life. I had no lifestyle, I was plain and simple. Then one day I witnessed something by sheer accident and I witnessed the same thing again in the same day and it got me wondering. It enticed me and I was lead straight to temptation for various reasons. Instantly my life changed and it began to bloom, not to mention I developed a lifestyle.

I didn't have anything or anyone to consider but myself and so I became comfortably enveloped within the escorting world. I won't go into depth or detail of what it entailed but it wasn't all what you may presume it to be. I reduced my working hours as a P. A. to part time in order to accommodate my escorting.

Then I met you.

You came along unexpectedly and I knew in my heart that I could never be with you. There was no way you could fit. I had no choice but to try and push you out. I didn't want to become attached to you simply because I never wanted to hurt you. I initially thought we'd be just a bit of fun as I had had no luck with relationships and had been single for a long time so it was no skin off of my nose.

It was skin off of my nose though.

You were everything I yearned for in a man, partner and companion. Caring, thoughtful, considerate, spontaneous, attractive, independent, hardworking, reasonable, approachable, fun . . . the list could go on.

I have an unwritten rule which I call the 'probation period' where after three to four months of getting to know each other it would become apparent whether it's comfortable to settle for the long term. Therefore I had a plan. I was going to keep my secret life from you for another couple of months and then when I was certain we were stable I would give it all up and dedicate my all to you. (It sounds silly, selfish and pathetic I know.)

It was cheating you, betraying you and being unfaithful but it was to protect you from hurt and to protect me from pain.

The night you confronted me as I left the Masquerade Ball is a night I will never forget. The cold night air against my skin causing me to shiver, the glow dimmed in you eyes and you left me standing all alone in the middle of the road with nothing but your exhaust fumes for company. (Nothing more than I deserved.)

I left the Masquerade early because that night I realised that I couldn't do it anymore, I couldn't hurt the people I loved and cared for and that was set as stone in my head as I left the hotel. As I left the hotel I left it all behind me.

But I never made it home, you caught me.

For what it's worth I'm truly sorry and no matter what you think of me I have no reason to hate you and so you will always have a special place in my heart. I understand if you wish you never laid eyes on me.

I believe the timing was wrong, but when is it ever right?

I just tried to make you understand.

Nina. Xxx

Aaron folded up the letter and put it back into its envelope and finished making Alec's hot drink.

"Goodnight uncle. For what it's worth I'm sorry." Alec said taking his drink and placing it on the dresser top.

"Everybody's sorry." Aaron said before saying his goodnight and preparing to take a shower himself.

He stood in the shower letting the water beat against his back and on to his shoulders. He closed his eyes and thought about Nina. She had made him understand but she hadn't stopped the hurting.

As he showered he envisioned Nina showering with him, lathered in soap suds, him kissing her juicy lips with her wet hair dangling over her eyes whilst he tried to grip her slippery curves.

He climbed into his bed and set his alarm clock for 7am and smelt Nina's scent on his bed t-shirt whilst he flicked through the photos of them both on his phone like he had done every night since they had split.

He loved her and he didn't know what to do about it.

JORDAN.

Jordan had left Mark a voice message asking if it was possible to meet up to discuss the house and their divorce. Mark had agreed but refused to go to the house, so they met up at TGI Fridays.

"Hi how are you doing?" Jordan asked Mark as he took a seat opposite her at the table.

"Fine." He replied, not even concerned about her well being in the slightest.

Jordan sensed his dismissive attitude and brushed it off as they ordered some food, neither of them were really that hungry and both wanted the whole thing to be over and done with as quickly as possible.

"I'm going to America with Nina and I don't know when I shall be back, if I decide to come back at all, so I shall leave it up to you to sell the house as I will be leaving in a couple of weeks." Jordan kept it short and simple.

Mark didn't respond in any way so she continued.

"I'll forward you the address I shall be staying at for correspondence and you also have my e-mail to update me on everything and what you may require on my part to progress with the divorce and the house."

Mark remained mute as he listened to her basic information, all the while wondering how it had come to this. He sat opposite her and felt as if he'd never known her at all, as if she were a stranger.

"Oh and lastly I am no longer with child, I had a miscarriage." She lied bluntly.

Still no reaction from Mark.

Their food arrived and they both sat in silence picking at what was on their plates. Eventually Mark spoke.

"I wish you all the best Jordan. Yes I'll deal with the house and you'll get your share don't worry." He said getting up and putting on his jacket. He threw a twenty pound note on the table. "You dropped something on the floor." He told her.

Jordan began looking down at the floor for what she may have dropped but couldn't see anything.

"What?"

"A tonne of guilt and lies that your trying to loose." He stated before leaving the restaurant.

As Jordan sat alone at the table in front of a pile of food she tried not to get upset and laughed to herself. "If I was still pregnant this would be a glorious treat."

She paid the bill and made her way home for a hot bath and an early night, she had work tomorrow, her students first set of exams.

NINA.

Every so often Nina kept glancing at her phone to see if Aaron had text or rung, as if she wouldn't have heard it make a noise. He should have received her letter that morning but she assumed he would have got it when he reached home from work that evening.

She lay amidst her pillows and cushions wondering why she hadn't heard from him yet.

"Perhaps he didn't understand or isn't interested." She told herself.

As she made herself comfortable re-arranging all her cushions and pillows her phone began to ring. Searching for it frantically in hope of it being Aaron, she eventually found it and Jordan's named flashed across the screen.

"What's up?" She asked Jordan.

Jordan told Nina about more or less the one sided meeting she'd had with Mark that evening.

"He just sat there like a statue. He agreed to sort the house out etc and passed a smarmy comment before he left. He couldn't even look at me for long Nina. It's as if we had never been married and shared a life together!" Jordan bawled down the phone.

Nina felt for her friend but really what did she expect?

"Don't cry Jordan, just think of all the exciting changes to come. Don't look back, life goes forward." She tried to cheer her up a bit.

She heard Jordan laugh a snotty laugh and smiled to herself.

"Goodnight Nina." Jordan whispered.

"Goodnight Jordan."

Nina was just drifting off into a deep sleep when she heard her phone beep. It was a text message from Mark telling her he needed to see her tomorrow about 6pm. She had a feeling it was about her and Jordan going to America.

28

AARON.

IT WAS 8:40AM as Aaron pulled up at Alec's college gates.

"Good luck, just do your best." He encouraged his nephew.

"Thanks for the ride I'll see you later." Alec said getting his bag off the back seat and shutting the passenger side doors before jogging along to the main entrance.

Aaron watched him to make sure he didn't take a detour. He was just about to drive off when he spotted Jordan pulling in to the car park. He parked up his car, not bothered about the time as he had informed his boss he would be a little late due to dropping Alec off for his exams. He got out of his car and made his way over to her. She had her back to him trying to retrieve her bags off of the back seat of her car.

"Good morning Jordan."

She jumped in fright nearly banging her head on the roof of her car.

She turned around, "Oh, Aaron it's you, you startled me. What do I owe this pleasure? It's been a while." She smiled at him. She couldn't remember the last time she had seen him. She waited for him to reply in hope of something good to pass on to Nina, after all why would he want to speak to her?

"I'll just get straight to the point Jordan, there is no pleasure."

Jordan screwed her face up a little, anxious at what he could possibly have to say to her that was so serious.

Aaron continued noticing her curious expression. "As you know, Alec is my nephew and I have just dropped him off to sit his exam. He's been staying with me this week and last night he told me everything."

Jordan's mouth fell open to the point of her not being able to close it back. She quickly looked away across the car park to see who was around. "It's not what you think." She started to explain, but Aaron wasn't interested.

"It doesn't matter what I think. I'm just letting you know that I am totally aware of everything that has occurred between yourself and my nephew, by that I mean everything. What makes this whole situation hard is that Mark has become a good friend to me and Alec is my nephew whom I will protect. I don't want to put a hurting on either of them so lucky you, your secrets safe with me." Aaron glared at her.

Jordan noticed his hazel eyes shine a piercing glow, quite similar to Alec's when he was angry. "I'm so sorry, I feel terrible, believe me I truly do. If I could turn the clocks back I would . . ."

"No Jordan, I'm sorry for your broken marriage and the loss of your unborn child." Aaron finished.

Jordan stood still, numb, trying to fight back her tears. "I have to go Aaron I have an exam to tend to." She told him locking up her car and making her way to the main entrance.

"Jordan!" Aaron called, "How's Nina?"

Jordan stopped in her tracks and turned around to face him. "She's missing you like crazy. We are both moving to America for a while. I'm not sure for how long. We leave in a couple of weeks." With that said she walked off.

Aaron got in to his car and sat, yet again scrolling through his phone looking at the pictures of Nina. His favourite one was of her posing in her bowling shoes holding the bowling ball with her hair all wild and curly smiling the most beautiful smile in the world.

NINA.

Nina had spent the day checking all the travel details for her and Jordan's trip and sorting out the rent for the storage place where she would be storing her furniture from her flat. She was so engrossed in her tasks she hardly noticed the time until her buzzer went off.

"Hellooo?" She sang.

"Nina, it's me Mark."

She buzzed him up and met him at her front door. He gave her a hug and kicked off his shoes on to the mat.

"Drink?" She offered.

"Yes thanks, whatever you got."

Nina poured them both a glass of cloudy lemonade with ice and they both took a seat on her sofa.

"So what's up then?" She asked him watching him fiddle with his glass uncomfortably

"Is it true you and Jordan are going to America?"

"That's correct." Nina confirmed.

"For how long?"

"We are not sure right about now, we'll see how we go. My brother is expecting us in less than a couple of weeks. Why?"

Mark didn't answer and so Nina poked him playfully. "Why Mark? What do you expect her to do?"

"Oh Nina, I don't know, this is all a big, fat mess! To be honest with you I met her last night to discuss the house and the divorce and I felt as if I didn't know her at all. I looked at her rambling on thinking; who are you?"

Nina laughed silently to herself recalling the phone conversation she had had with Jordan the night before. She didn't know what to say, there was nothing left to say, nothing could make the situation any better. Each one of them just had to get on.

Mark gave up and changed the subject. "Have you heard from Aaron?"

Nina felt tender at the mention of his name. "No. I wrote him a letter which he should have received by now. I tried to explain why I did what I did but it seems as though he isn't interested, so what more can I do? I tried. Sometimes I question what I would do if I were him?"

She looked at Mark in case he had an answer.

Mark held her gaze and instead of providing her with an answer he put his drink down and brushed the side of her face gently before kissing her passionately.

Nina pushed him off of her, "Mark!" She screamed, "What the hell do you think you're doing?"

"Nina it's you. I love you, I always have and I don't want you to go. It's you I'm going to be lost without. Aaron's a fool if he doesn't want you."

Nina couldn't believe her ears and what had just taken place. She sat in shock suddenly feeling uncomfortable in Marks company.

"Mark, every single one of us are a bag of jumbled emotions right about now. Nobody knows what they are feeling or what they want and that's the reason I have decided to go away. For some time out. I'm sorry but I don't feel for you the same way and I'm going to America no matter what." She told him.

Mark sat feeling awkward and rejected. He left Nina's with his head down.

29

BEEP! BEEP! BEEP!

Nina rolled over and turned the alarm off on her phone. It was 7am Friday morning and she had a lot to do. Tomorrow morning her and Jordan would be at Gatwick Airport, boarding their flight to Atlanta.

Nina, Jordan and Claire were going out that night for a meal at Jimmy Spices and a few drinks to celebrate a new beginning, but before that Nina and Jordan had to go through their to do list to ensure everything was in place and ready for there departure.

All of Nina's furniture was in storage so she was stopping over at Jordan's. Mark had kindly offered to take them to the airport. It was more for convenience so he could collect the house keys off of Jordan and silently, secretly say goodbye to his love.

Nina was quite happy with the plans as they were all being civil to each other and would have the opportunity to say goodbye. It was a pity Aaron hadn't come around.

"I'm just going to hand my flat keys in to my landlord and say goodbye to Mr Allen!" Nina shouted from the bottom of the stairs to Jordan, as she tied her laces on her Keds.

"No probs!" Jordan shouted back to her from the bathroom.

Nina got to her empty flat and wondered around reminiscing. She sat on the floor of her empty closet remembering how and where she had placed her shoes and clothes. She looked out of her bedroom window laughing to herself as she used to stand there everyday looking up at the sky to decide what to wear to suit the weather. Before she left she stared at the spot in the hallway where the shoe mat once lay. She blinked tears away as she thought about Aaron's Adidas trainers lying next to her Prada's. Those damn Pradas.

"Nina!" Mr Allen stood up from behind his desk to embrace her. "When do you leave?"

"Tomorrow morning." she told him smiling, grateful to be around such happiness.

"Are you all packed and ready?"

"Ready as I'll ever be." She laughed, automatically straightening the stationary on his desk.

Mr Allen slapped her hands away playfully, laughing at her obsessive behaviour.

"I can't believe I'm saying this but I'm going to miss you and this place." She sobbed.

"I'm going to miss you to." Mr Allen said handing her a gift bag he had pulled out of his desk drawer.

"You shouldn't have."

"Oh yes I should. You have been an asset to me, the team and this business and I have no choice but to show my gratitude. It is well deserved."

Nina opened the bag to find an expensive pen with her name engraved on it.

"Thank you very much." She said kissing his cheek, "This will be my lucky pen." She laughed.

Nina returned to Jordan's house a couple of hours later and for the rest of the day they spent their time looking on the internet at the exciting things Atlanta had to offer them. It wasn't long before they were making themselves pretty like Princesses for the night ahead.

Both ladies met Claire at Jimmy Spices on Broad Street. Nina had told Claire to pretend to be her work colleague (which was true in a sense) because Jordan was still unaware of the secret life she had lead. Claire agreed, she didn't care, just so long as she got to see Nina before she left.

The girls stuffed their faces. They must have gone up at least four or five times, each filling their plates sky high with onion bhaji, somosas, massala fish, Thai green curry, chicken korma, a range of salads and not forgetting desert. They drank plenty and left the restaurant tipsy and carrying their bellies to the next destination.

They stumbled up Broad Street, arms linked and made their way in to Roccoco Lounge to dance the night away.

"I'm going to miss you gorgeous lady!" Claire shouted in Nina's ear above the loud music, kissing her on her cheek.

Nina laughed and kissed her back, "I'm going to miss you to you mad woman!"

Ne-yo's, 'Come Closer' came on and Jordan screamed out for Nina to join her on the dance floor. "Woohoooo! Our song!"

Claire leaned against the wall and watched as Nina and Jordan did their dance. Every now and then she'd holler, "Go girls!" Pumping her fists in the air in her drunken state. Everyone circled them to watch them dance and some people even tried to participate. Nina was shocked when Jordan began grinding with a random guy.

"Go Jordan." She giggled.

After a fantastic night out the girls fell into a taxi dropping Claire home first before reaching Jordan's and collapsing on Jordan's bed in their party frocks, falling asleep and snoring like a pair of pigs.

"Come on girls, wake up otherwise you'll miss you'll flight." Mark tapped them.

"Oh my gosh!" Nina jumped up startled.

"What time is it?" Jordan groaned.

"Time to get up and get ready!" Mark shouted at her impatiently. "The showers running, hurry up, you have half an hour. We'll stop off at McDonalds on the way to pick up some breakfast." He laughed as he watched them drag themselves up and into the bathroom.

"I bet your heads are POUNDING!" He shouted at them.

"That's not funny Mark!" Nina told him off.

"Hurry up I'll meet you in the car."

With that he left them to get ready and took a couple of their cases out to the car.

No longer in the happy mood from the night before, hung over and tired, the girls dragged the last cases out to the car. As they loaded the trunk a silver Audi A3 pulled up on Jordan's drive.

Aaron stepped out of the car.

Nina suddenly froze and stared at him.

Jordan and Mark did the same.

"Are you ok?" Jordan asked Nina noticing the little colour she had drain from her face.

"Y . . . ye . . . yes I'm fine." She stuttered.

Jordan and Mark stood apart from each other and leaned patiently against the car to see what Aaron wanted.

Nina privately refused to make her way toward him.

She waited and watched as he strolled her way. His face was expressionless therefore Nina had no idea what to expect from him. She shivered in the chilly morning air, her stomach churning.

As he got a little closer she noticed the glint in his hazel eyes and his hands tucked into his jeans pockets, just like the night they met when he walked her to her door. She began to smile subtly as she noticed him doing the same.

Mark leaned forward up off the car so he could hear what Aaron was about to say.

Jordan stayed positioned, yawning.

"Nina, I'm sorry I took so long but I couldn't sort out how I felt about you. I got your letter and Mark and Jordan told me you were going to America . . ."

"It's ok Aaron. I did wrong, I don't expect you to forgive me, I'm just glad I have the opportunity to say goodbye to you before I leave."

"No Nina, you don't understand. I hope I'm not to late."

"What for?" Nina asked all confused.

At this point Jordan and Mark walked up a little closer and stood by Nina's side facing Aaron, also confused.

"I love you Nina. I love everything about you. I got your letter. Since we have split up I have spent everyday looking at your photos on my phone, missing you and wanting you."

He got down on one knee and pulled a jewellery box out of his jeans pocket.

Jordan gasped and Mark shook his head.

"I have all this love for you and it's suffocating me. I need to give it to you. Nina, will you marry me?"

Lightning Source UK Ltd.
Milton Keynes UK
UKOW04f2309250315

248550UK00001B/195/P